HEARTS DIVIDED

**Center Point
Large Print**

**This Large Print Book carries the
Seal of Approval of N.A.V.H.**

HEARTS DIVIDED

FRANCINE RIVERS

CENTER POINT PUBLISHING
THORNDIKE, MAINE

To Tom and Carol
In appreciation for their selfless efforts
in the preservation of our home town

This Center Point Large Print edition
is published in the year 2006 by arrangement with
The Berkley Publishing Group, a division of
Penguin Group (USA) Inc.

L.T.E.
Rivers

The text of this Large Print edition is unabridged. In other
aspects, this book may vary from the original edition. Printed in
Thailand. Set in 16-point Times New Roman type.

ISBN 1-58547-751-6

Library of Congress Cataloging-in-Publication Data

Rivers, Francine, 1947-
    Hearts divided / Francine Rivers.--Center Point large print ed.
        p. cm.
    Novel.
    ISBN 1-58547-751-6 (lib. bdg. : alk. paper)
        1. Large type books. I. Title.

PS3568.I83165H43 2006
813'.54--dc22

2005031208

Chapter One

Carla Gelsey entered the meeting room quietly and took an inconspicuous place at the back where she could work out plans for her project. Her mouth tightened as she overheard the conversation going on around her. Glancing up, she listened more attentively.

She had heard groups like this one before, and they never failed to earn her contempt and arouse her anger. "Out with the old and in with the new" was their motto, and they would do anything—even tread on a nice, defenseless old lady like Mary Weatherby—to modernize their town.

Weatherby House was now under informal discussion by members and visitors of the Allandale City Council. The meeting had not yet been called to order, but excitement was high as everyone awaited arrival of the planning council chairman, Blake Mercer, who was also Mary Weatherby's great-nephew. He would give the report on the status of Weatherby House.

Carla leaned back in her metal folding chair and crossed her slim denim-clad legs. The man with the gavel must be Mayor Frank Suraco. He met Mary's description of a man with great nervous energy and the "flibbity-gibbits." He was speaking:

"Well, tonight should put an end to this whole discussion, but I can't help feeling a little sorry about Mary. She's lived in that old house for decades."

"Sorry?" asked a plump lady in a tailored navy-blue

dress, offset by three strands of pearls beneath her pale jowls. Her lips pursed. She was the only woman in the room with "persimmon-colored hair" and, therefore, must be Cynthia Seder, wife of the local banker.

"Oh, Frank, for heaven's sake," she went on. "The house should've been condemned years ago. It's probably rotten with termites. And that horrible garden! Why, half a dozen criminals could hide there in broad daylight, and no one would know. I'm scared to death to pass the place at night on my way home from these meetings."

Carla thought Cynthia Seder looked capable of freezing any criminal with a single down-the-nose stare.

A small, wiry man with gray hair and horn-rimmed glasses fit Mary's thumbnail sketch of George Talbot. "It does seem ironic that right next to us here at City Hall is the worst eyesore in Allandale. Why, we've been slaving for five years to give this community a proper facelift, and there's the biggest pimple!"

Cynthia's brows lifted like warm bread from a toaster.

Suraco cleared his throat. "Well, we've got good news tonight. Weatherby House has been the last hitch in the plans, and Blake has smoothed things over. After we tear it and this old building down, we can begin putting up the new civic center, which will make us proud."

Several men were sitting near the front. The youngest, dressed in a western shirt and denims, winked at Carla. With an inward sigh she lowered her head and continued her computations. She had plans to make, people to contact. She wouldn't even be at this ridiculous meeting if Mary Weatherby hadn't begged her to come. Carla hadn't quite decided how best to come to the point of her attendance.

"If only Mary hadn't wasted all this time," Cynthia complained, glancing at her diamond-and-gold watch. "Where's Blake? It's almost eight."

"He's driving up from Sacramento after his own company board meeting. He'll be here soon," Suraco said, turning his pencil like a windmill on the table.

The door swung open and Carla glanced up. A tall, athletically built man in an expensive-looking three-piece brown business suit entered the meeting chamber. Her eyes widened as she took in the chocolate-brown hair that swept a broad, tanned brow, the straight nose, firm mouth, and square jawline. Then she met the darkest, most arresting brown eyes she had ever seen, and felt the man's open declared interest before he strode by. Her heart thumped crazily, and she swore to herself that she could feel the surge of energy that followed in his wake.

"You'll know Blake when you see him," Mary had said with a faint smile. She was right.

Carla watched him walk to the front of the room, take his place at the long table, and set down his briefcase. His bold, half-smiling gaze touched her again. Slipping her pen into the spiral binding of her notebook, she tipped her chin and lifted one brow.

Suraco was smiling. "Good to see you, Blake. We can

get on with it now." He quickly called the meeting to order and asked for committee reports. While various chairmen spoke, Carla could feel Blake Mercer watching her intently. She was a stranger among these people, but when she again encountered his eyes, she knew he was more interested in her waist-length auburn hair and blue eyes than in her reasons for being here. On second thought, and third look, she decided that it was probably her scooped-necked, fitted T-shirt, or what lay beneath it. Color heated her cheeks as her mouth tightened.

When Suraco called for Blake Mercer's report, the room grew noticeably hushed. This was what everyone was waiting to hear. Mercer stood up. He was brief and to the point, like an expert shot firing on a clay pigeon.

"As we discussed at the previous meeting, the papers have been drawn up and presented to Mary again. She almost gave her consent and signed the agreement yesterday, but then she asked that I wait until tomorrow morning."

Cynthia sighed audibly in exasperation as others murmured impatiently.

"I know she's done this before," Blake went on with a wry smile, "but she assured me she's ready to sell. The place is too much for her to handle, and she's at an age where she needs some outside care. She no longer has a choice about the house."

Carla was liking him less and less.

"Then you're sure she's going to sell?" Suraco asked, excited.

"Absolutely. With Mary's signature and Chuck Seder's full cooperation, everything could be settled within the month."

Cynthia smiled broadly. "Charles will be more than happy to speed up escrow."

They all looked as pleased and smug as hogs on a manure pile, Carla thought, as she listened and watched from her unobtrusive position. Not one person in the room raised a single objection.

"It's best for Mary to sell," Suraco said, nodding. "She's eighty-four now, and her health has been failing for years. She can't possibly see to that big old place, and she certainly hasn't the income to fix it up so that it'd be presentable. I don't think anyone has."

Blake Mercer opened his briefcase and took out a rolled sheet of graph paper. "I've made some preliminary sketches for the new civic center. If you like them, I'll have a model made up for next month's meeting."

He tacked the large sheet up to the bulletin board behind the long table. Everyone leaned forward excitedly to see it. Carla heard general murmurs of appreciation and approval.

It was definitely modern, she thought grimly. The lines were simple. The new building was designed to house three times the number of business offices the present hundred-year-old brick building contained, and it would also have a large auditorium available for convention groups. Weatherby House and this grand old hall would, of course, be torn down to make way for the elegant new building. Blake Mercer assured everyone that two or three days with a crane and bulldozer would be enough to accomplish that task.

Carla seethed.

"I think the design is absolutely marvelous!" Cynthia Seder bubbled, jowls quivering. "It has distinction, yet a modesty of line."

Others agreed, praising Mercer's architectural genius. "It's exactly what Allandale needs to put us on the map," said the young man who'd winked at Carla.

She could remain seated, and silent, no longer. She set her notebook aside with a crack and stood up. "May I address this august committee?"

Surprise met her request. Suraco glanced question-ingly at Blake, who smiled and said, "If the lady will kindly introduce herself first." His gaze moved over her with open appreciation, which brought amused smiles to numerous onlookers.

"Carla Gelsey," she supplied without hesitation, meeting his gaze with cool disdain.

"You had some comment to make?" he asked with a raise of dark brows.

"A few comments, yes. But to preface them, I lived briefly in Allandale some years ago," she informed everyone with a sweeping look around the packed room. "One of my fondest memories, and one that brought me back here, was Weatherby House. I used to stand at the gate and admire the house."

Cynthia Seder gave another audible sigh. "Please get to your point, young lady. We've plenty of business yet to finish."

Carla ignored her. "When I lived here before, Allandale boasted six buildings of historic interest. I've been informed that the Gingham Palace Hotel burned down, but that Knott's Feed and Grain, McGathey's Hardware, the Saint Ignacio Catholic Church, and the Grange were all torn down to facilitate this committee's idea of a community facelift.

"Now I hear you all plotting the same sad demise for the last two buildings of any historic value in this area, Weatherby House and City Hall!"

She had their full attention now, and could feel the hostility emanating from a dozen pairs of eyes. Blake Mercer's had narrowed sharply. She looked around again with unveiled accusation and challenge, then settled on Mercer himself. Ignoring the tension that was building between them like a tangible force, she gave him a mocking smile.

"Frankly, Mr. Mercer," she said, "in my opinion Weatherby House is the only building in this town worth saving. And that"—she pointed at his plans tacked to the board—"is about as interesting as a stack of supermarket apple boxes."

There were audible gasps and then a loud rumble of anger. Amazingly, Mercer seemed amused by her insult.

Suraco pounded his gavel for order, but Carla shouted over the uproar: "I'm not quite finished!" In fact, she was just beginning. "Allandale was a gold-mining town one hundred and thirty some years ago, and what you propose as an *improvement* is little better than the blight of glass and steel that's cropping up all across our country. It's about as appropriate here in Allandale as a bullfrog singing in Carnegie Hall!"

A dozen people shot to their feet and shouted to be recognized. Blake Mercer's face was enigmatic as he sat down and leaned casually back in his chair. He was probably expecting everyone to tear her apart, Carla thought. His cool gaze moved slowly over her in thorough appraisal, from her jeans upward, lingering on her T-shirt once again, which was emblazoned in white against black: NON ILLEGITIMUS CARBORUNDUM—Latin for "Don't let the bastards wear you down." She wondered if he knew his Latin or was just assessing her body beneath the stretch fabric. Angry color crept up her neck and into her cheeks.

Suraco recognized a muscular man with graying hair. He stood and turned to glare at Carla, informing her hotly, "This hall has ten city offices in which to squeeze all the services of our town of over twenty-eight thousand. The heating system is archaic and air conditioning is nonexistent. It gets cold in the winter and hot in the summer. How would you like to work in this place when it's a hundred degrees outside and hotter inside?"

A young woman stood next. "And as for that old house, it's falling to pieces. Tearing it down would be taking a burden off an old woman who hasn't been able to cope with it for years. It might have been something long ago, but now it's just a mess!"

Suraco pounded his gavel again, but he was rapidly

losing control of the meeting.

"It's an embarrassment to our community!" someone shouted.

Mercer's expression clearly said, You're getting exactly what you deserve for sticking your nose in where it doesn't belong.

Carla smiled at him. "Weatherby House is structurally sound. It can be restored."

Voices grew even louder. "Restored!" some cried. "You're out of your mind, lady! It'd take a fortune and years to do it!"

Forcing her gaze away from Mercer's mesmerizing dark eyes, Carla addressed the general gathering: "Weatherby House could be rehabilitated in less time than it would take to build anything like it again. As for cost, that would depend entirely on who did the work," she added, trying to appear calm in the face of rising tempers.

She heard grumbles of, "Who is she, anyway?" "Why doesn't Frank tell her to shut up and sit down?" "Thank God, no one wants to renovate the old dump!"

A heavyset, middle-aged man in a blue workshirt was recognized by a harassed Mayor Suraco. "What're you suggesting, lady? That Allandale raise funds to fix that place up? For what? As some kind of historical point of interest?"

A poodle-permed woman in a green jersey dress stood without being recognized by the mayor. "I'd like to make a comment about your insensitive remark! Blake Mercer just happens to be one of the country's leading architects, and one of his buildings would be appropriate anywhere!"

Suraco pounded his gavel again, beads of sweat standing out on his pale forehead. He glanced at Blake Mercer pleadingly, but got no help.

"To answer the gentleman's question," Carla said clearly, "I'm not suggesting anything. I'm merely stating my opinion."

"Well, keep it to yourself!" someone shouted.

She went on doggedly. "I returned to Allandale because of what I remembered about it. It was a charming, friendly town with a Gold Rush flavor. I can't tell you how sorry I am to see that so many historic buildings have made way for what you all seem to believe is progress. I would hate to see this town changed entirely."

"As would we all," came Blake Mercer's deep, calm voice. He stood and the room full of people fell silent. Eager pairs of eyes looked from Carla to the big powerful man at the front of the room. Blake Mercer wore a patient, condescending smile. Carla could see that everyone expected him to put her in her place—which would be out of this meeting.

"This isn't one hundred and thirty some years ago, and the needs of Allandale aren't the same as they were then," he explained. "I can't speak for the other buildings you mentioned, but as for this one in which we're now meeting, there's little to recommend it as an historic landmark. Granted, it's old, but old doesn't make it historically significant. As for Weatherby House, it's

14

too run-down to warrant the cost of renovation." He paused and gave her a half-smile.

"Now I'm sure an intelligent young woman like yourself will agree that our town needs a larger administrative building."

Blake Mercer was just the kind of patronizing male chauvinist Carla despised. She had met more than enough of them in her life.

"Indeed," she agreed, "but you needn't destroy what little town history remains in order to build one."

His smile was sardonic. "History remains, whatever is torn down, Miss . . . Kelsey, was it?"

"*Gelsey,* Mr. Mercer. With a *G,* as in *guillotine.* Allandale won't have any visible history for those passing through. It'll look like a hundred other unremarkable places on the map without Weatherby House or this hall to commend it."

"If you feel that way, why don't you go someplace else!" an angry voice burst out, and there was smug laughter and hissed agreement.

She smiled sweetly. "I'm here for the duration, ladies and gentlemen. Allandale became my home this afternoon."

"Well, we're sorry you feel as you do, Miss Gelsey," Mayor Suraco said, having regained his composure. "But this issue has been under consideration for some time. Five years, in fact. Everything has been settled."

Carla drew in her breath. "I'm afraid not," she said quietly. "You see, Mary Weatherby sold her house to me late this afternoon. She informed me of your plans

15

and asked that I attend this meeting and share my own intentions with you."

She let the stunned silence settle for a second before lunging on to give her final punch. "I plan to renovate Weatherby House myself and open a bed-and-breakfast inn sometime within the next eighteen months."

With her announcement made, she picked up her notebook and walked out of the meeting room.

Chapter Two

Weatherby House stood on a large city lot right next to the square, two-story, brick building of City Hall. A rusted wrought-iron fence surrounded the property, and the house was barely visible through an overgrown garden of fruit trees, hedges, roses, and weeds. Once past the gate and ten feet into the yard, Carla could see the house itself.

Three stories of Victorian rose into the star-jeweled sky. It hadn't been painted since the early 1950's. The gingerbread was decaying in places, and two front windows on the upper level were badly cracked. The roof had been recovered with asphalt shingles rather than wood. Ten sagging steps led up to a veranda that stretched around the front and south sides of the house. On the south was an ornate solarium, an obvious later addition.

Carla could understand how the townspeople might come to the mistaken conclusion that Weatherby House was not worth repairing. Yet with her trained eye Carla knew the house had great possibilities. Even if it had been rotten with termites, she would still have bought it, for she'd dreamed of living here ever since her first sight of it as a seven-year-old child.

Besides that dream, Carla needed a project to help her forget the dual tragedies of the past two years—the death of her parents and the betrayal of her fiancé.

Refocusing her thoughts, she glanced at the house's seasoned redwood foundation, noting again that there was some damage of dry rot. There was work to be done in the high eaves and outer walls as well, and the roof would have to be stripped entirely and redone with proper wood shingles. What Weatherby House really needed was hard work and tender loving care—and she could give it both.

The oak door, replete with dust-covered stained glass, opened. Mary Weatherby stood just inside the foyer, leaning on her cane. Her face was deeply lined, but the china-blue eyes sparkled.

"What happened?"

Carla smiled wryly and entered. "I'm not sure. I retreated before they could lynch me, but I heard something like a sonic boom when I closed the door behind me."

"Oh, dear me," Mary murmured, turning around with an effort and preceding Carla into the parlor. She put the cane aside and braced her slight weight as she gingerly lowered herself into an old wing chair, which was badly in need of recovering. The room was paneled in

17

dark wood and appeared drab at first glance, but Carla knew that a treasury of antiques was hidden in the shadows.

"You're sure you still want to take on this project?" Mary asked, a worried frown crinkling the small oval face framed by fuzzy white hair. "You've seen now what you'll be up against."

Carla blushed guiltily. "Mary, I'm afraid I was a bit premature. I told them that I already bought the house this afternoon."

Mary Weatherby beamed and began to chuckle. She leaned back. "You're just what the doctor ordered, Carla."

Carla sighed heavily. "We're in for trouble."

"Indeed! Oh my, to have seen their faces when you announced your plans to renovate the house. Did you also tell them what you'd like to do with it when you're finished?"

"Yes."

"I can see you gained a certain amount of satisfaction from that little disclosure." She grinned. "I think we're a lot alike, Carla. You enjoy stirring people up a bit, too, don't you?"

"When things need stirring up. Too many historic buildings are being bulldozed to make way for high-rises."

"You're sure you won't mind having an old woman underfoot while you're working?"

"I thought you wanted to stay." Carla frowned.

"Oh, yes, I'd love to stay until I die in my own bed,

but I can't really expect you to take on any responsibility for me, no matter what we discussed this afternoon."

"Mary, I gave you my word," Carla told her firmly. "And I'm going to hold you to yours. When people come to stay here, they're going to want to meet you and talk about how things were."

"A hundred or so years ago," Mary said, another grin spreading across her charming old face. "I'll become one of the antiques they come to see."

Carla laughed softly. "And you'll have wonderful stories to tell them just like the ones you shared with me."

"Oh, indeed, I will. Why, did you know that when my grandfather, Michael Weatherby, brought his young Bostonian blue-blood bride to live here, he already had a mistress living upstairs. He was a man of great forethought." She giggled wickedly. "And the parties he used to give were—"

She was interrupted by the loud peal of the front doorbell. Someone was leaning on it. Mary smiled demurely and folded her hands in her lap. "That will be Blake, of course, and in one of his tempers from the sound of it. You'd better go answer, Carla."

When Carla opened the door, Blake Mercer stormed past her before she could open her mouth to protest. He strode into the parlor and stopped in the middle of the room, hands on his hips as he glared down at his sweetly smiling great-aunt.

"Just what in hell is going on around here, Aunt Mary?"

Mary smoothed her skirt. "I've been given to understand you already know, dear."

She reached casually over to the round, marble-topped side table and picked up a large packet of papers, which she handed ceremoniously to Carla. "There you are, Carla. All signed, sealed, and delivered."

Carla opened them quickly and scanned to the last page.

"You can't do this!" Blake growled.

"I can and I have," Mary responded simply. "Oh, I know what you wanted, Blake. Five minutes after I signed your papers, you'd have had me out of the house and that bulldozer of yours roaring in my front yard."

"This place should come down, and you know it!"

"I know no such thing!"

Blake's face was stiff and pale. "Will you kindly explain something to me, Aunt Mary? Why did you tell me yesterday that you'd soon sign the papers to *our* agreement? You've never broken your word before."

Mary's face pinked. "I didn't exactly break my word. I said I was ready to sell. And I was. Carla only arrived yesterday after some weeks of exchanging letters. I wanted to meet her in person and talk with her. Now that I have, I know she's the answer to all my prayers."

Blake cast a furious glance at Carla. "And just who is this Carla Gelsey?"

Carla was too ecstatic over her good fortune to be properly tactful. She held up the papers and waved them. "As of this moment, I'm the proud owner of Weatherby House!"

"Not quite, you're not," Blake snarled through gritted teeth, glaring down accusingly at his now red-faced great-aunt. "Or didn't you bother to explain the entailments—"

"Now don't be difficult, Blake," Mary interrupted hastily. "Admit you've been outfoxed, and we'll settle that issue between us."

He snorted. "There's only one way I want to settle it, and you know it," he told her. "Just out of curiosity, what did you get for the place?"

Mary told him, and he blanched. "We offered ten thousand more than that!"

"*And* I have a place to live in my old age," Mary added. "I can remain here in my own home until I die. You know very well you expected me to sign myself quietly into that old folks' home on Vineyard Avenue," she told him with a sniff. Her mouth pursed in distaste. "You know I loathe knitting lap rugs and bedroom slippers, or playing bingo, and that's all they do out there— except perhaps discuss their latest bowel movements."

"Good lord!" Blake muttered. "You can't stay here forever, and you know it. If you don't like that retirement home, pick another more to your liking."

"I've picked and I'm staying."

Blake ground his perfectly straight white teeth. "Aunt Mary, I think you've finally lost all your marbles. You can't really believe this place is worth saving. We've been through this a hundred times. It'd take the outside of a hundred thousand dollars to do it. Maybe this fool here doesn't know that, but you do!"

"It'll take about fifty thousand dollars," Carla interceded smoothly from her safe vantage point at the fireplace.

Blake gave her a scathingly contemptuous glance. "You're either stupid or an idealist. With labor what it costs, you're as far out of your head as my great-aunt here is!"

"Now don't be so rude, dear," Mary admonished, her lips twitching. "You'll have to forgive him, Carla. He's always been able to speak his mind with me, but as you can see for yourself, he doesn't think clearly when he's mad." Her eyes twinkled merrily as she glanced back at her great-nephew, who seemed momentarily unable to speak at all. "And besides, Blake, you don't know the entire story."

"Then suppose you fill me in."

"Carla just happens to be a licensed general contractor."

Two full seconds passed without a sound. Then Blake spoke in a low, menacing growl. "A *what?*"

"A licensed general contractor with a master's degree in architectural design." Carla answered for herself, wishing this man's magnetism didn't make her senses respond like a quarter-activated pinball machine.

"That's just terrific," he said and gave a sharp, derisive laugh. "I suppose you plan on rehabbing this place all by yourself."

"No. I have several friends whose help I plan to enlist." She smiled tauntingly.

Another prolonged, steaming silence passed, broken

finally by Mary Weatherby's chuckle. Blake looked at her and then back at Carla. She was grateful he kept his thoughts to himself. Mary grinned more broadly, unruffled by her great-nephew's wrath.

"They'll be moving in soon, won't they, Carla?"

"Very soon."

Blake said something beneath his breath that brought a stinging flush of anger to Carla's cheeks. In her own behalf, she added, "I'm just short of earning my Ph.D. in Victorian restoration."

"Have you ever been involved in restoration—outside the classroom?"

"Yes, extensively. In San Francisco."

"How extensively?"

She blushed. "One year."

"*One* year?" He let out an angry breath. "It's getting worse by the minute."

"I don't have to explain anything to you, Mr. Mercer," Carla told him fiercely, giving vent to her own Irish temper. "But to ease your simple mind, I know what I'm doing!"

"I doubt that very much, Miss Gelsey!"

"Time will tell," Mary put in gaily, looking from one to the other with amusement. "Why don't you sit down, Blake? It makes my neck ache having to look up at you."

"I'm not in the mood to sit! I'm more in the mood to string you both up by your thumbs! What do you expect me to do about my part in this . . . this . . ." He gestured sharply around the room.

"You and I can discuss that," Mary interjected and glanced uneasily at Carla, who frowned.

"I suppose you just figured I'd sell my ten percent as well," he muttered.

"Sell your ten percent of what?" Carla asked, glancing between aunt and great-nephew with growing trepidation.

Blake glowered at her as Mary rolled her eyes heavenward. "My share of Weatherby House," he said. "What else? Or didn't you even bother to research all the documents on the house?"

Carla paled and looked at Mary for explanation. The old woman gave her a faint smile and spread her arthritic hands. "I'm afraid that's one little something I forgot to mention during our discussion, Carla," she said apologetically and then looked at Blake reproachfully.

"You'd better explain it now," he told her sternly.

"Couldn't we just—"

"No, we could not."

"Oh, *all right.*" She sniffed indignantly and faced Carla again with a wan smile. "My brother and I each inherited half of Weatherby House. Peter didn't give a hoot about the house, but he knew very well how much I loved it. I"—she cleared her throat—"committed a few . . . indiscretions as a young lady . . ." Blake gave a sharp laugh. Mary's eyes twinkled. "And Peter felt he could exert some major control over me, and make a tidy sum at the same time, by agreeing to sell out—but only in ten percent increments every five years. Peter passed on before he really had a chance to try dictating my life. But then I inherited Blake's father, every bit as much an autocrat as *his* father *and* his son!" She grinned at Blake. "He thought he'd hold the reins for some years, but sadly he died in a plane crash near Bakersfield. And now we have Blake with his ten percent."

Carla could not hide her dismay. Blake smiled grimly. "With four-and-a-half years to go before I have to sell it," he finished.

"How much do you want for it?" she asked solemnly. Somehow she'd raise the money, she decided fiercely.

"I'll offer you that same price I did my great-aunt. That's a clear profit of ten thousand dollars in one day," he said incitingly, eyes dark.

"And what about Mary?"

"My great-aunt can take her pick of any retirement home she likes, and I'll see to her continued support."

Mary looked up at Carla with wide, vulnerable eyes. In Carla's own mind there had never been a moment's doubt about what she wanted: Weatherby House! It seemed Mary was still certain as well. Carla met Blake's cold look. "Sorry, I'm not interested."

Mary beamed. "I knew I wasn't wrong about you!"

"Obviously, Miss Gelsey, you're no businesswoman." He pointed at her. "I'll warn you now that I'm going to fight you. This place is coming down."

Carla's temper erupted. "Oh no, it's not! And I'm businesswoman enough to know you have a conflict of interest. Tell me, Mr. Mercer, how did you manage to make yourself chairman of the Allandale planning committee when you're part owner of property under discussion? If that isn't enough, you're also proposing to design and build the projected administrative building! That's as flagrant a conflict of interest as I've ever heard!"

"Oh dear," Mary murmured.

Carla took a step forward, not yet finished. "You try to block me, and I'll take court action against you!"

A muscle was working in Blake Mercer's jaw, and his dark eyes were like black coals as they held hers for a moment. Then, without a word, he stalked out of the room. The front door slammed violently and feet pounded down the front steps. A few seconds later the iron gate clanked. A powerful car roared to life and screeched away.

Mary looked at Carla with quiet gravity. "My dear, you have all the tact and diplomacy I ever did." Then she leaned back in her chair and chortled.

Chapter Three

Carla's first order of business was to make half a dozen long-distance telephone calls to line up her work force. She knew whom she wanted and kept her fingers crossed that they would all be available and willing to come on her terms: free room and board in exchange for their expertise.

Marvin White, a carpenter she'd met while working in San Francisco, was out of work and fast running out of money. He agreed readily to her proposition. He'd be in Allandale within the week, providing his much-loved but highly overworked VW van could make it.

Michael Divalerio was in the middle of a battle with his employer. He was grateful for the opportunity to tell his boss to take his job and shove it. "This jerk wants me to remove the gingerbread because it'd cost too much to sand and paint it!"

"It'll be some time before we're painting Weatherby House, Mike. I need you for jacking it up and replacing basement beams that have dry rot. We'll worry about the cosmetic touches later."

"Your say, lady. I'm on my way."

Michelle Tibadeaux was also eager to come. She'd recently been laid off her job at a rehab project in Sacramento due to lack of funding, and was looking for something to keep her going. Of course, she'd come. Would it be all right if she brought her son, Jacque, with her? She couldn't trust her ex-husband to keep a proper eye on the boy. Carla agreed. How much trouble could a four-year-old boy cause?

Next Carla dialed the number for Sam Lierow, a classmate from Berkeley. She knew he had been involved in some restoration of post-World War I houses in West Oakland. She had also heard from friends that he was recently out of work and just divorced.

"I owe you a favor, Carrie," he agreed. "I'll be there with bells on."

Two others Carla called were working on projects and couldn't come. A third was getting married at the end of the month. Carla crossed her fingers and dialed the last number on her list.

Roger Deveritch was really a sculptor who had had several important showings at well-known galleries in the Bay Area. Unfortunately, his art couldn't support his expensive life style, so he did the decorative plastering on restoration projects from time to time to pay past-due bills.

Carla had met him when she was an apprentice for a San Francisco architectural firm involved in restoration. He was lying on a scaffolding like Michelangelo doing his plaster magic on a ceiling. She watched him work with admiration. He had found much to admire in her, too.

They had dated steadily for several months without becoming seriously involved. Carla had seen from the beginning that Roger was a rogue, and she knew he made a steady habit of sleeping with his numerous nude models. Eventually they became good friends instead of lovers. In fact, it was Roger who'd first introduced her to Rob Hanford, which turned out to be one of the great disasters of her life.

Carla dialed Roger's number. "Ah, darlin', I'm due for a change of scene," he said when she explained her situation. "Blondes, blondes, blondes. But tell me, where in Hades is Allandale? I've never heard of it."

"About a hundred miles from you, Rog. East on 80, then south. If all else fails, buy a map at a service station. They're only a dollar."

He laughed softly. "Carrie, you've a heart of stone.

Anybody interesting going to be there . . . besides you?" She smiled in amusement, hearing the teasing, seductive quality in his voice.

"Oh, two others."

"Where am I sleeping?"

"On the second floor with a couple of other men. You remember Sam and Marvin."

"Where will you be?"

"Top floor. I'm the boss."

"Carla Gelsey, you're a heartless woman, but I'm still in love with you, darlin'. When're you going to forgive my wandering soul?"

"I forgave you long ago, Rog, just as soon as I realized I was far too much woman for you anyway," she teased back. He made an insulting remark about female general contractors, and she laughed. "Just come and work for a month or two . . . or three . . . and I'll be forever indebted. But please, Rog, keep your hands off the local girls."

"You know I never make promises I can't keep," he quipped and hung up.

Carla relaxed back in the old wing chair and tossed her pencil on the notepad with satisfaction. Her work force would be gathered at Weatherby House within the week. Exhilaration filled her. She wanted to get started right away.

Mary was sitting in the rocking chair on the veranda. A confession magazine lay open in her lap, and her wire-rimmed glasses were perched halfway down her pert nose. She glanced up at Carla's approach and

29

grinned. "How're your plans coming, dear?"

"Perfectly, but the real work will have to wait a few more days." She glanced around at the overgrown garden. "Mary, have you any gardening tools? I might as well get started somewhere."

"My, you're an eager little beaver." Mary beamed, setting her magazine aside. "There'll be some things in the shed, I imagine, though it's been years since I used any. You'll need the key to get in. It's hidden in a teacup on the top right shelf of the china hutch in the dining room." She frowned slightly. "At least, I think that's where I last put it."

Carla found it there and noted that the teacup mentioned so casually was priceless antique Havilland china.

Inside, the shed was dark and booby-trapped with spider webs. Upon careful investigation, Carla found a pair of rusty hedge trimmers, a broken hoe, a short-handled shovel, some ancient clippers, and a cane rake with half its teeth missing. She went back around the house to Mary.

"I'm going to buy some tools," Carla said. "Most everything seems to have been removed or broken."

"Oh dear. Well, Joe Brady has a hardware store on the corner of First and Main. He should have everything you need."

Carla found the store with ease and parked her three-quarter-ton pickup out front. She recognized the man behind the counter as one who had been at the meeting the evening before, and from his baleful countenance it was obvious that he remembered her as well.

She found the items she needed and brought them to the counter. She laid down hoe, rake, four extension cords, an electric hedge trimmer, a lock, and a pair of gloves. "I think I'm going to need three of those large garbage cans you have over there as well, please."

Brady tallied the total on his computerized register and watched as she wrote out a check. She tore it off and held it out. He shook his head. "Sorry, I don't take personal checks."

"I have a guarantee card."

"We don't have that bank in this town."

She breathed in slowly as she tore up the check and voided the amount on her stub. Then she pulled a charge card from her wallet.

"Don't take that either," he told her, arms crossed over his chest. Carla put the card away and tapped a sign on his counter that said: ALL MAJOR CREDIT CARDS ACCEPTED. He turned red.

"Mr. Brady, I'm going to be living in Allandale, and I'd much rather buy what I need from you than go elsewhere. I'm going to need a circular saw, two large disc sanders, and a pneumatic hammer, but I don't carry that kind of cash around with me. I prefer using a credit card so I have a clear records of business expenses." Already she could see his pupils had enlarged at her list. "I'd rather not go to the chain store down the road," she went on, "but if you—"

"On second thought, your check will do just fine, Miss Gelsey, and the card for the rest."

Next she bought groceries from a small corner store and was relieved to find the middle-aged woman loquacious. She didn't even ask to see Carla's identification.

When Carla returned to Weatherby House, she put the tools in the shed, then brought two loaded bags of groceries up the back steps into the large country kitchen. When she finished putting the groceries away, Carla pushed through the swinging door into the dining room.

"Mary?" she called. It was almost noon and she wanted to ask Mary what she preferred for lunch: soup and a sandwich or a chef's salad.

"Mary?" Carla entered the parlor and froze, swift color mounting in her cheeks and a jolt of sensation tightening her stomach as she saw Blake Mercer standing with his arm resting casually on the mantel. He was dressed in slacks and a light green polo shirt that accentuated the breadth of his chest and the narrowness of his waist. His brown eyes collided with her blue ones.

"Come in, Miss Gelsey," he drawled with a provocative smile, gesturing for her to sit down.

She glanced at Mary's grave face in hesitation. "Am I intruding, Mary?"

"We're discussing the house," Blake informed her.

Carla gave Blake an impatient glance, but his expression was grimly enigmatic. She walked across the room and sat down on the faded mauve sofa by the front windows, aware the whole time of Blake's gaze following her.

She lifted her brow mockingly. "Do go on, Mr. Mercer," she challenged.

His mouth tightened, and he gave her a curt nod. "I was just trying to explain the concept of eminent domain to my aunt." Carla froze. "Are you familiar with the term?"

Anger rose swiftly in her. So you're going to play nasty after all, are you, she thought, seething.

She looked at Mary's confused face and smiled calmly. "Basically, Mary, it's a legal method used by a city to purchase and then destroy private property at will." Then, very dryly and with a telling glance at Blake's rigid face, she added, "All for the community good, of course."

"That's not completely accurate," he objected.

"It's true, however. I've seen it in practice more than enough times to know."

"If this is the kind of building project you've been working on, that's small wonder!"

"It has less to do with the building than with the small-minded individuals who are too quick to rip everything down so they can put up their block-and-steel highrises!"

"Oh, dear me, are we going to have another argument?" Mary murmured, her china-blue eyes dancing.

Blake glared at his great-aunt with unconcealed impatience. "I know you're loving this mess you've created, Aunt Mary, but since you're no longer directly involved, would you mind staying out of it?"

It was less a question than an order. "By all means,

dear," Mary demurred and Carla smiled, which only served to further incite Blake Mercer.

"As for you, Carla Gelsey, I want a few words with you in private."

The very idea of being alone *anywhere* with this man alarmed her. He was far too masculine, and the way he had studied her at City Hall the night before, the way he had broadcast his interest in her from head down, was extremely disturbing. Those same eyes were now taking in the motto on today's T-shirt: VENI, VIDI, VICI! From his dark expression, she knew he understood Julius Caesar's "I came, I saw, I conquered!"

"A bit premature, aren't you?" he growled. "In the library. Now."

Sighing, she stood slowly, trying to appear calm and indifferent to his anger when her insides were churning with nerves. "All right. We might as well get this settled."

Carla preceded Blake out of the room, down the hall, and through double doors on the right into the shadowed library. The room smelled musty. Blake yanked the doors closed, and Carla put as great a distance between them as possible. Pulling the tattered drapes open, she let sunlight stream in through the graying Nottingham lace. Blake's deep, angry voice accosted her from the other side of the room.

"By your own admission you haven't been in Allandale in years, yet you march right into City Hall, smug as you please, and tell us what we ought to do with this town. You obliterate plans the city council has been working on for five years and fan grievances that have been around even longer than that! All this in barely twenty-four hours! Just where in hell do you get off, lady?"

She maintained her bland expression with difficulty. "My, my, but you're in a temper, Mr. Mercer, and all because of my definition of eminent domain."

"Your closed-minded definition didn't surprise me one bit. I expected as much from you."

Her blue eyes narrowed to angry slits. "I don't happen to think much of you either, Mr. Mercer, or of your tactics; but then it shouldn't surprise me at all that someone as progressive as you obviously are wouldn't think twice about harassing an eighty-four-year-old lady, even if she just happens to be your own flesh and blood!"

A muscle worked spasmodically in Blake's firm, square jaw. His brown eyes blazed as he pushed his hands deeply into his pockets, obviously concerned that if he left them free they might find their way around her neck.

"That nice old lady you're so concerned about would be a match for an entire regiment of United States Marines!" His mouth tightened at her soft, disbelieving laugh. "My great-aunt Mary has always enjoyed stirring up trouble. Half her reason for clinging to this old fire trap is the enjoyment she's getting from all the excitement. She's got everyone on the council taking high blood pressure pills!"

Carla tipped her chin. "I admire her spirit. She knows

the value of Weatherby House, and she has no intention of letting anyone bulldoze it *or* her!"

Blake walked toward her, menace in every footstep. "Another earthquake and Mother Nature will take care of the demolition Herself," he retorted. "This place will come down around both your ears!"

"The structure is sound."

Blake said something impolite about her intelligence, and since Carla had heard it before when dealing with men in her field, she didn't flinch. In fact, she gave him an amused, condescending smile.

"There was quite a discussion in City Hall after you dropped your little bomb last night," he told her.

"Ah, I'm sure there was."

"Eminent domain was just one of the things that came up."

"At your suggestion, no doubt."

"As a matter of fact, it wasn't," he said, smiling coolly, his gaze dropping over her slowly and lingering on the motto across her full breasts. "I said you looked like an intelligent woman."

Carla blushed. "I'll just bet you did," she muttered.

He smiled more warmly, noting the deep color in her cheeks with obvious amusement. "There was also some mention of rezoning and hitting Weatherby House with a high-density-business tax. They've held off out of respect for Mary."

And obviously not for me, Carla said to herself. "Will this tax apply to everyone on Main Street, or just the owner of Weatherby House?"

Blake took a few more steps toward her, and Carla tried to ignore the pace of her heart. He had entirely too much sexual magnetism for comfort, and she didn't like the sensual way he was regarding her.

"You'll have to check on that for yourself," he remarked easily.

"I've a few tricks of my own. I'm well aware of all the devious methods used to try and force people off their property, and I can fight back. If you try the high-density tax on me, I'll file for present-use tax relief. It's been used before when big corporations moved in and tried to gobble up small family farming concerns. It'll serve my purpose as well. As for the rest," she went on tightly, "if you're going to play nasty, then I will too."

"How?" he challenged.

She sucked in her breath. "Allandale is dependent on federal funding for its major building project. If you try to block my restoration of Weatherby House, I'll contact a few friends in high places about drying up this town's money. Take *that* back to your city council and let them smoke it for a while!"

Amazingly, Blake grinned. "You know the weapons to employ," he drawled, "but do you expect to make any friends in this town by using them?"

Unfortunately, Carla had no answer for that question. She sighed heavily, embarrassed at having lost control so easily at his baiting. Just what was it about Blake Mercer that grated on her nerves? She looked up at him and was hit again by the force of his dark eyes. Her mouth tightened.

"I didn't come back to Allandale to make enemies or do battle, Mr. Mercer."

"I'm glad to hear that, and call me Blake." His slow smile sent tingles from her toes all the way up to her hairline, and warning bells went off in her brain.

She glared at him. "Is this sudden charm another tactic of yours?"

"Anything's worth a try."

There was too much self-confidence oozing from that caressing look to merit an answering smile from her. "It won't work."

"Oh, come on. Be reasonable. Why don't I take you to lunch, and we can talk about the situation like two adults?"

"Thank you, no. I plan on having lunch with Mary."

"Mary has already had lunch. She was finishing it when I arrived. So much for that excuse."

"The answer is still no."

"No fraternizing with the enemy? Why not? Are you worried I might get you to change camps?"

"Over one lunch? You've a colossal ego." She laughed derisively.

"How about dinner too?" He grinned. "Actually, I credit you with being intelligent enough to weigh all the facts. There are some things you obviously don't know, things I'd like to explain."

"Explain away."

"It's past noon, and I'm hungry, Carla."

"All right, *Blake*. Go eat your lunch and come back later."

He gave an exaggerated sigh. "Since you aren't going to be civilized about this, I'll try to sum it up for you now." He took her arm, leading her forcibly to the sofa by the bookshelves, and pushed her down onto it. His eyes glinted with laughter at her indignation. "We might as well be comfortable," he drawled, and sat down next to her.

She shifted to put more space between them. "Get to the point."

His mouth curved wryly as he rested his arm on the back of the couch and said, "Six years ago, two major businesses moved out of Allandale and set up shop closer to the Bay Area. Each of those two businesses threw two hundred people out of work here. Now that may not sound like much to you, having come from San Francisco, but to Allandale it meant depression. Those workers had to find other jobs and when they couldn't, they had to put their homes up for sale in order to leave and go elsewhere. Without enough businesses to bring new people in, those houses didn't sell and there were foreclosures."

She frowned in comprehension. It wasn't a new problem.

"The situation doesn't stop there, as you know. It's a vicious downhill spiral. Local merchants feel the pinch. The schools have a decreased enrollment and, therefore, a drop in government funding. And so on and so on. Are you beginning to get the picture, Carla?"

"I understand the problem, but I still don't agree with your solution. How do you think ripping down the last two historical buildings will change all that?"

"Putting up new buildings creates jobs," he said patiently. "It's rudimentary."

She had faced this kind of logic before. There were good arguments on both sides. High-density business buildings in downtown areas brought renewed life to a city, but the historical landmarks gave the townspeople a sense of pride and roots, as well as revenue. Unfortunately, Blake's logic all too frequently won out and historical landmarks were knocked down and built over. Once that was done, the buildings were lost forever. All that remained was a memory of past glory and a marker that said: ON THIS SITE STOOD THE HOME OF . . .

Carla couldn't let that happen to Weatherby House. "When it's all done, what's left of the old Allandale? Nothing. Just a lot of new construction."

"The buildings in question here don't have all that much historic value, Carla," he said in irritation. "This place has a certain charm, sure, but not enough to warrant the cost of rehabilitating it and then keeping it up. And City Hall is little more than a square brick box."

"That's a matter of opinion," she informed him stiffly.

He let out his breath. "Just like most preservationists, you care more for an old house than for living people."

"It's for the present and future generations that we need to preserve places like this!" she argued hotly. "This is part of Allandale's heritage, whether you like it or not."

"What good is it if the town dies?" he demanded sharply. "If something isn't done to bring new blood

40

and business into this town again, there won't *be* an Allandale in ten years!"

Her blue eyes sparkled. "Is it really Allandale you're so worried about, or that administrative building you'd like to put up?"

He stood so abruptly that Carla jerked back in fright. "Lady, that's the second time you've insulted my integrity." He glared down at her. "I lost my temper last night, but this time I'm not walking out. I'm going to straighten you out on a few things."

She swallowed hard as he bent over, pinning her against the sofa with a hand on either side of her shoulders. "Those plans I made were a suggestion based on what the members of the council said they wanted for Allandale. I'm getting no commission for the design, and if any money's forthcoming, the job will go to another general contractor." He straightened. She breathed again.

"Very magnanimous," she managed. "And the general contractor . . . one suggested by you, of course," she dared.

He gave her a cold, tight smile. "Probably," he admitted. "Since I'm in the construction business, I could make some sound suggestions for honest men who could get the job done properly, and in a minimum of time."

"No doubt," she said, and then wondered why she wanted to incite him further.

"Someone close to the area who would be willing to hire *local* labor for the project!" Incited he was.

Her heart raced at his closeness as he bent down again. She wished he would move away instead of standing so close that she could feel the brush of his hands against her shoulders and see the strong muscles of his thighs through the smooth material of his slacks. He moved restlessly, and sensation shivered through her.

Then he stepped back and said, "The town needs this property as well as the land on which the City Hall sits to proceed with the project. The offer we gave is fair market value, plus a little, considering the condition of the place."

As soon as space allowed, she got up and moved a few feet away from him. "Now that you've had your say about the matter, may I have equal time?"

Hands on hips, he looked at her with ill-concealed impatience. "Go right ahead."

"I've sunk everything I have into this project because I believe in it. Weatherby House is one of the most beautiful Victorians I've seen."

His expression mirrored disdain and she went on stiffly. "It should be an historical landmark, and I plan to have it put on the national registry as such."

"Good luck, but that won't save it."

"It's worth the try. If this town will only give me a year to eighteen months, I can rehabilitate Weatherby House and open it to the public. They'll be proud of it."

He gave a sharp laugh. "Eighteen months! You're a dreamer! Five years wouldn't be enough time to do it. And if you've sunk everything in already, you haven't the money to even start phase one, let alone two or three, in the renovation of a place like this!"

"Eighteen months," she repeated with confidence.

"They won't wait."

"*They* won't wait, or you won't let them?" she challenged.

He advanced on her again, brown eyes darkening. "Your personal attacks have come once too often," he said through his teeth. "What's in this for you, Miss Gelsey? A purely altruistic concern for posterity and future generations?" he sneered. "Hell, no. You're in this for your own personal interests. You don't care about anyone, just as long as you get your chance to experiment. You're not even worried about ripping off an old lady of ten thousand dollars!"

Carla gasped. "That's not true!"

"Isn't it? You sized up the situation like a pro. You took advantage of your quarry's weakness with that offer of letting my great-aunt stay here indefinitely."

"I didn't know about the city's offer," she insisted, face pale. "I offered Mary everything I could afford and still have the funds I needed for the project. And she *will* stay here, just as long as she wants."

"While you're ripping the place inside out and upside down with your rehab efforts?"

"That's up to Mary, not you! The idea didn't alarm her in the slightest."

"Because she has no idea what she's in for, that's why, and you, most likely, didn't bother to enlighten her!"

Carla drew herself up to her full five feet, seven inches. "I explained everything to her. *In detail.* I told her what would be going on! And I didn't come here to rip anyone off!" Her hands clenched at her sides. "I offered what I could, and Mary accepted because she loves this house and wants to see it restored to its former glory."

Some of the anger dissolved from Blake's face as he studied her intently. "She never will," he said softly. "I think you're an impossible dreamer, Carla Gelsey." He shook his head solemnly. "Just because a house is old doesn't mean it has any historical value or that it's worth saving."

"Weatherby House is worth saving," she said firmly, though she knew she would have to prove its historic value.

"There're a hundred others like it within fifty miles of Sacramento, and most are in better shape. Why don't you sell out and use your profits to buy one of them?"

"What about Mary?"

"I'll take good care of my great-aunt."

"Sorry, I'm not interested," she repeated. "I want Weatherby House, not something like it. I also made a promise to Mary, which I fully intend to keep."

His eyes teased. "I almost wish you luck, but I'm afraid you're doomed to disappointment." He held her gaze intently, and her stomach tightened with warm awareness. His expression grew enigmatic and watchful. "We'll be talking again soon, Carla," he warned, and left.

Carla breathed out slowly, but it wasn't so easy to control the racing of her heart.

Chapter Four

Marvin White was the first of Carla's crew to arrive in Allandale. He immediately earned the public ire when his Volkswagen van died in the middle of Main Street and traffic was halted. There was consternation when he got out to push the vehicle and people took full note of his long sandy-brown ponytail and full beard. That consternation grew when Carla came flying out the gate and threw her arms around him in greeting. Yet the real public furor began when she helped him unload his suitcases and portable stereo system and ushered him into Weatherby House as though he were visiting royalty.

"Friendly town," Marvin commented dryly.

Carla grinned at him in understanding. "Don't worry, they'll get used to you soon enough."

Mary's blue eyes widened in surprise when she got her first look at Marvin, but his easy charm and polite manners quickly won her over.

The next two crew members to arrive were Sam Lierow and Michael Divalerio. Sam was small and wiry with a receding hairline and shrewd eyes behind wire-rimmed granny glasses. Michael Divalerio was tall, well built, and darkly handsome with a sultry romanticism that drew interested glances from local

45

girls and worried frowns from the adults. Again citizens noted suitcases being unloaded. Again eyebrows rose.

Two days later, petite Michelle Tibadeaux arrived in her Indian muslin dress and Arabic sandals with her son Jacque in tow. They moved into the first floor, down the hall from Mary.

Roger called to say he couldn't come for another couple of months, but work would begin at Weatherby House immediately.

To anyone watching from the outside, nothing was going on inside Weatherby House but hanky-panky. Yet downstairs in the basement trouble lights were hung about and backs were straining, sweat was pouring.

"A couple more inches," Mike grunted. A combined effort of muscle and hydraulic power got the house jacks in place. Thick beams were slid into position.

"All right!" Mike shouted exuberantly and the others cheered and slapped one another on the back. Carla took off her white hard hat and wiped that sweat from her face. The real work was only just beginning, but she loved it.

Michelle appeared in the doorway. "Lunch!" she announced. "Come and get it!"

Everyone washed up in the kitchen and then filed into the dining room. There was a big bowl of tossed salad, a selection of dressings, a tureen of French onion soup, and a platter of sandwiches. Everyone dug in, famished from their morning's labors.

"It's going well," Sam told Mary between bites. "I don't see a lot of dry rot. It shouldn't take us long to replace those sections that need it."

"I want to scrape every board and beam and make sure we aren't overlooking any dry rot," Carla told them, sipping hot coffee.

"Gees, Carrie!" Mike groaned.

"It shouldn't take us that much longer." She smiled at him.

Everyone cleared their own dishes, leaving them on the counter for Carla to wash later. She'd drawn first K.P. Then they went back to work. For the next three hours the high scream of a circular saw filled the basement.

For the next week Carla scraped wood, checking each beam and board carefully and chalking those to be replaced. By mid-afternoon each day she was covered with dust and grime. Her back ached, as did her arms and hands. Mike worked behind her, prying out damaged wood, while Sam and Marvin measured, cut, and refitted boards into position.

"That's all the lumber we've got, Carrie," Marvin announced one afternoon shoving his protective goggles up on his head and shutting off the saw. Carla straightened up and rubbed the small of her back with a leather-gloved hand.

"Okay. Let's shut down for the day."

"What do you want us to do with all this?" Mike asked, indicating the pile of damaged lumber.

"It can be cut for firewood later. Just leave it for now."

Mike grinned. "Thank God. I thought you were going to crack the whip and ask us to do it tonight!"

"Well, if you're volunteering . . ." She grinned.

"No way!"

She laughed. "You guys go on up. The showers are yours first." As she turned around, she saw Blake lounging against the doorjamb, looking her over. She stiffened defensively as her heart took a sharp leap.

Marvin glanced at the door. "Hi. I take it you're not here to help," he commented, nodding toward Blake's suit.

Carla yanked off her gloves. "This is Blake Mercer, fellas. He's head of the planning committee that wants to tear this place down."

Blake grinned at her. "I came to see how the work was going."

She spread her hands casually and gave a faint shrug. "Take a look-see, if you like."

Marvin, Mike, and Sam filed up the stairs, looking Blake over with a mixture of speculation, hostility, and curiosity. Carla introduced each of them as they left, but only Marvin offered his hand, which Blake shook firmly.

Blake remained where he was after they left. A faint smile played on his lips as he took in her full appearance.

She was only too aware of how she must look in her grimy jeans and workshirt. Sticky with sweat and covered with sawdust and dirt, she felt like the village hag. Sawdust had filtered into her shirt, where it made an itchy plaster. For just that reason she never wore a bra when she worked.

Blake's immaculate gray three-piece suit, pale blue shirt, and dark silk tie made her feel even worse. He was the business executive right down to his expensive leather shoes. She glared at him resentfully, waiting for the typically chauvinistic remark she was accustomed to hearing from men when they saw her on the job.

"So you don't object to pitching right in with your men," he observed. It sounded like a compliment.

"It *is* my project," she clarified, watching him warily as he came down the steps. He loosened his tie and unbuttoned the top of his shirt as he looked around with a cool, professional eye. He was noting the placement of house jacks, the evidence of scraping and chalking of damaged sections, and the pile of discarded lumber.

"You've accomplished more than I expected," he told her frankly.

She resented the rush of pleasure his remark gave her. Why should she care whether he approved or not? "I told you—eighteen months," she reminded him.

Blake moved closer. Her heart started to thump rapidly. He was looking her over again, and the slow perusal sent tingles spiraling downward from the pit of her stomach. She blushed. He grinned.

"You know, I think I like you, Carla Gelsey."

"Thanks," she muttered ungraciously and turned away to pick up her white hard hat. "Have you seen enough?" she asked without looking at him again.

"Of the work down here, yes. Of you, no."

She lifted her head sharply. His brown eyes were having an alarming effect on her equilibrium.

"Why don't you let me take you out to dinner this evening?" he suggested.

She gave him an exaggerated look of derision. "I'm not exactly ready for an evening out."

"I'll wait for you to shower, shampoo, and change into a dress."

Assuming she wanted to wear a dress, she thought mutinously. "Thank you for the invitation, but I'm busy." She was wary of the response he could arouse in her with just a simple look.

His eyes lit with amusement. "I think your friends would let you out for the night."

"If I wanted to go out, I'm sure they would," she agreed with a wry smile.

He reached out and brushed some sawdust off the end of her nose, and she started at his touch. "What're you afraid of, Carla?" It was a soft challenge and one she didn't appreciate. He caught her wrist as she moved to turn away. "We've a few things to discuss, and I thought it'd be more pleasant if we did so over a nice dinner, rather than having another confrontation in the library." He was teasing her.

She drew her wrist firmly away and looked up at him defensively. "More bad news, I take it." She meant it to sound flippant. It didn't.

"Some."

She sighed wearily. "What now, Blake? A vigilante committee?"

"You're not too far off."

She stared up at him and saw he was actually serious.

"Well?" He raised his brows. "Are you going to have dinner with me or do I leave you hanging?"

"You've such a wonderful way of getting a woman's acceptance," she snapped.

"I tried the other way." The dark eyes danced. "I don't usually have to resort to tough tactics. In fact, I think this is the first time I have."

Carla marched toward the stairs. Her hand on the electrical switch, she glanced impatiently back at him. He was still standing in the basement, his suit jacket now off and slung over his shoulder. He was grinning up at her.

"Are you coming, or shall I leave you down here in the dark?"

"You go on up," he said. "I'll shut down for you. I want to look around a little more."

"Oh, no, you don't," she told him firmly. "I'll wait right here until you're finished."

He put his hand to his chest theatrically. "You don't trust me."

"Why should I? You've made your position perfectly clear. You'd probably jam the jacks or break something."

"You don't think much of me, do you, Carla?" It was said lightly, but there was grimness in his eyes. They narrowed and assessed.

"No, not much," she agreed bluntly.

He walked up the stairs. Her breathing stopped as he did on the step just below her, bringing them eye to eye. He was so close she could see the faint gold flecks in his irises; the dark, long lashes; the faint shadow of his beard. He wore a heady aftershave. He put his hand up over hers where it remained on the switch. She tensed and tried to draw her hand away, but his tightened.

"You can trust me, Carla. I don't use underhanded tricks. I fight right out in the open."

Her heart was beating wildly. Why did she have the feeling he wasn't just talking about Weatherby House? His gaze dropped to her mouth.

Oh God! I don't need this, she thought frantically. Not after Rob Hanford. She didn't want to be attracted to another man. Blake Mercer was altogether too dangerous. Even Rob had never aroused this kind of trembling awareness deep inside her.

Blake was watching her closely, a faint smile on his lips. He came up the last step, and she drew in a sharp breath and backed away a step. She could feel his body warmth. He tugged her hand down and shut off the lights.

Darkness closed around them, and Carla jerked her hand free of Blake's. Before she could turn, she felt his hands at her waist.

"Careful," he whispered and turned her toward the kitchen and light again. When he released her, she let out a tremulous sigh of relief. She moved quickly away from the gentle hand on her hip.

"I'll be with my great-aunt. Just give a knock on her door when you're ready to go," he said as she headed for the swinging door, wanting to get away from him.

"All right," she muttered.

"Carla."

She glanced back, face pale, mouth tight. His eyes were warm. "I'm in no hurry."

Chapter Five

Carla stood beneath the shower for fifteen minutes. The warm water had long since given out, but the cold hard spray was refreshing, and she let it pound down on her aching muscles while noting that the tiled stall needed regrouting.

She stepped out and rubbed herself vigorously until her skin was warm and tingly. Then she wrapped the towel around herself and began blow drying her long, auburn hair. She kept it braided and twisted up under her hard hat while working so that it wouldn't get caught in the machinery. Brushing it slowly, she took a full half hour to dry it.

She wondered if Blake was patient, or if he was grinding his teeth like most men who were forced to wait for a woman. Maybe he'd give up and go home.

She selected a simple green-and-gold silk dress with a slit at each side of the narrow skirt. After slipping on high-heeled sandals with delicate straps around her ankles, she glanced in the mirror. A quick touch of blusher, eyeshadow, and lip gloss and she was ready.

Just below, Marvin's stereo was playing Rachmaninoff. She went down the stairs and along the hallway. When she tapped at Mary's door, there was no answer. She smiled slightly, thinking Blake had gone after all.

Then a burst of laughter came from the parlor. Perhaps Mary was holding court there, sharing one of her infamous ribald stories with the crew. She'd go back up and change before joining them.

She was halfway up the stairs when a man cleared his throat in the foyer below her. With a glance back, she saw Blake standing at the bottom step, his hand on the banister. He smiled as his gaze traveled from her nylon-clad legs up over her slim hips to her loosely flowing hair.

"*Very* nice," he said softly. "Did you think I'd left?"

"It occurred to me," she managed, and turned around to come down again. "I'm sorry you had to wait so long."

His mouth twitched. "I knew you'd get tired of stalling sooner or later. If not, you'd get hungry. Actually, you came down sooner than I expected. I gave you two hours."

"I'll have to remember that the next time."

"Don't you mean, *if* there's a next time?"

She felt her cheeks sting with heat. He laughed softly at her embarrassment, his hand lightly caressing the sensitive skin along the inside of her upper arm.

"There *will* be a next time, Carla. You can bet on that."

Not if she could help it! "Where's Mary?" she asked, to change the subject.

"In the parlor. She's telling your friends about the mistress who lived upstairs." He put his hand on the small of her back. "Wish her good night and let's go."

Mike Divalerio gave a wolf whistle when Carla appeared in the doorway. *"Mama mía!"* He kissed his fingertips and, while the others laughed, gave a fine performance of heavy breathing. No one seemed surprised or disturbed to see Blake with his hand around her waist. In fact, Michelle looked at Carla with an expressive approving lift of her brows.

Mary was sitting in her wing chair. She smiled smugly at Blake. "Where're you taking her?"

"Tomaso's," Blake announced.

"Oh, don't take her there! It's too dark, for goodness sake. You can't even see what you're eating."

"Maybe food isn't what Blake has on his mind," Sam said with a leer at Carla.

Mike grabbed Michelle's arm and began planting passionate kisses from her wrist up to her shoulder as she pretended to swoon. Carla gave them all a fierce stare.

"Take her to Sterling's," Mary ordered. "It's so much more elegant."

"I was thinking of someplace a little more intimate, Aunt Mary," Blake said frankly. "Someplace where we can . . ."—he glanced at Carla's stony face—"talk. We need to get to know one another better."

"Watch out, Carrie." Mike laughed and gave her a bawdy wink.

"Will you please shut up?" she hissed at him.

"Treat him nice. Remember, our fate is in his hands!" Mike said, grinning broadly.

Blake chuckled. "I'll remind her of that, Mike." His

hand tightened on her hip. "Your chariot awaits, milady," he said gallantly, then glanced at the rowdies giving them a bad time. "Don't wait up, folks. We may be late."

Carla was almost grateful when they left the house. The cool night air was a relief on her hot face. She glanced resentfully up at Blake. "You certainly made friends with them fast enough." She knew they wouldn't have teased him otherwise.

"I'm not such a bad guy once you get to know me."

She pushed the iron gate open before he could and stepped out onto the sidewalk. A sleek, dark green Jaguar was parked at the curb. Blake opened the door for her.

She looked the car over before getting in. "It's very nice, but infinitely impractical for a general contractor."

"I have a truck for the job site. This is just for cruising Main."

"So all the local girls can say *far out*," she added, and couldn't suppress her own amused smile at the thought of Blake Mercer driving back and forth on Main Street. It was too incongruous.

The car purred to life with a flick of Blake's wrist, and he turned it into the light traffic. She ran her hand over the black leather seat. "You must be doing very well."

He glanced at her and grinned. "There's more money in steel-and-glass apple boxes than in preservation."

"Too true. Is that what matters to you? Money?"

"In your words, I believe in my projects. I believe in

the buildings I design and put up. They're earthquake- and fire-safe, make the most of limited space, are interesting to look at, and will last three times as long as any Victorian riddled with termites and dry rot."

Carla could feel her blood pressure rising and was sure that was exactly what Blake wanted.

"What?" he drawled. "No comment?"

"You know my sentiments."

"Ah, *sentiments*. That's an excellent word."

She clenched her hands in her lap and swore to herself that she wasn't going to argue with him.

Blake let the silence lie until they reached the small Italian restaurant tucked in a pinewood canyon. He turned off the ignition and then leaned back, his arm resting on the seat behind her. Her tension mounted. The car was too small, and she felt caged. She was self-conscious as she felt his intent gaze move over her.

"I apologize for baiting you," he said softly.

She could read nothing in his dark eyes, but she trusted neither his capitulation nor his gentleness. She was responding far too quickly to his potent virility. His closeness, their small shared space, and the faint scent of his aftershave were heady. She preferred his quick temper, sarcasm, and patronizing attitude to this charm and sensuality.

"Let's get something straight in the beginning, Mr. Mercer," she told him softly, hands still clenched in her lap. "If you brought me out here to threaten, lecture, or coerce me into selling Weatherby House, then you're wasting your time and mine."

57

His smile was faintly mocking. "You're far too defensive with me, Carla. Why?" He brushed her shoulder lightly with his fingertips, and she couldn't prevent her tremor at the sensation it caused. "Am I really such a threat?"

"I don't like to play games," she said stiffly.

His eyes narrowed. "Neither do I." He opened his door and got out. She had already opened her own and was standing by the car when he came around.

"You could allow me to do the courtesies," he said dryly.

"Why? I don't have a broken arm."

"No, but I lost an opportunity to get a good look at your legs."

She felt her face burn with angry color. He took her arm and led her firmly into the restaurant.

Tomaso was a middle-aged man with black hair and a broad, toothy grin. He looked as though he greatly enjoyed his own pasta. An enthusiastic handshake greeted Blake, and a dark-eyed, admiring look passed over Carla.

"Bellisima," he said and kissed his fingertips.

Blake laughed. "This is the lady who bought Weatherby House right out from under my nose."

Tomaso bent low over her hand. "Then I salute you." He glanced at Blake. "I have just the table waiting for you. It's the one you requested." He winked.

Carla found herself seated in a small, private cubby at the far end of the restaurant. It was very quiet, and there were windows around her so she could look down over the small creek that ran through the canyon. Soft pastel lights illuminated the area, and she saw that platforms of food had been put out for the wild animals. A deer and fawn were approaching cautiously.

"Oh, look," she whispered, pointing, pleasure filling her at the sight.

"If we're lucky we'll see raccoons as well. There's a whole family of them," Blake informed her. He murmured something to Tomaso and the man departed.

She straightened and looked across the table at him. They were here for a reason, and she had better remember it. "You had something to tell me," she prodded.

"Relax, Carla. We've got all night."

"Hardly all night."

He smiled slowly. "A mere slip of the tongue. Don't panic."

"I came because you told me—"

He gave her an impatient look and sighed. "You don't relax your guard for a moment, do you? All right. We'll get business out of the way first, and then talk about something else for the rest of the evening."

It was on the tip of her tongue to ask him what they could possibly have to talk about *other* than business, but she desisted. There was no use deliberately antagonizing him. It wouldn't help her position at Weatherby House, or in Allandale.

Tomaso appeared with a carafe of red wine and a basket of warm French bread. He poured two glasses, then departed.

"May we have a toast before we begin?" Blake requested.

She lifted her glass. "To the restoration of Weatherby House and a better Allandale."

His mouth curved in wry appreciation. "And to the end of hostilities between us."

She eyed him warily over the rim of her glass. Just what was he up to? All this charm wasn't for nothing.

He set his glass down and grinned at her. "I can almost hear that overactive brain working. Suspicious, touchy . . ." He shook his head.

"Will you please get to the point?"

"Directly." His eyes were filled with amused devilry. "Some of the citizens of Allandale think you've started a hippie commune in Weatherby House."

Her eyes widened; her lips parted. "A *what?*"

"A hippie commune."

"Are you serious?" she muttered, disbelieving.

"A dozen or more people saw Marvin arrive and move in. I'm afraid that with his ponytail and van . . ."

"Marvin just happens to be one of the best carpenters in the business!" she defended him hotly.

"And then Sam and Mike and Michelle and her son arrived," Blake went on lazily. "There's been a general panic in town ever since."

"I suppose they think we're having wild orgies day and night!"

He gave her an interested grin. "Are you?"

"Did it look like it in the basement this afternoon?" she retorted stiffly.

"I wouldn't know. Anything could have been happening before I arrived on the scene. Some people think a pneumatic hammer has erotic overtones." She knew he was teasing, but she was too annoyed and distressed at what he had just told her to take it all so lightly.

"What else are they saying?" she asked dismally.

"Oh, there's been a lot of general talk going on up and down the streets of Allandale," he went on laconically. "Someone suggested we call in the vice squad and raid the place. Another thought you should be run out of town on a rail. A few others suggested organizing a group to throw firebombs and take care of the problem of Weatherby House once and for all. You see, they're very worried you and your friends might corrupt the young people."

Carla couldn't help laughing. It was all too preposterous.

"You've made their week, Miss Gelsey," Blake added after a moment. "They haven't had this much excitement in ten . . . no, I take it back . . . thirty years."

She grinned unrepentantly. "And what happened here thirty years ago?"

"Aunt Mary had a little too much champagne at her birthday party and was seen netting goldfish in her pond. I believe she was wearing her birthday suit, or so the story goes."

Carla gasped with laughter. "You're serious?"

"Would I lie to you, Miss Gelsey? She had apparently scooped out a dozen or more by the time the sheriff arrived. I should remind you that in those days the garden wasn't overgrown and the pond—and Aunt Mary of course—were within plain sight of the entire Main Street."

"I can't believe she'd do it." Carla giggled.

"That's because you don't know Aunt Mary. But you will . . . given some time."

"Why on earth was she netting the fish in the first place?" she asked, filled with curiosity.

"That I couldn't begin to tell you." He smiled wryly. "You'll have to ask her, if she can even remember. But knowing my great-aunt, I'd guess she was just trying to shake everyone up and give the town a little excitement."

"She must have accomplished that." Carla took another sip of wine and raised her brows. "Where is the pond? I don't remember seeing it."

"Aunt Mary had it filled in and covered over shortly after the incident. The town fathers breathed a collective sigh of relief, knowing she'd be unable to repeat her performance. She'd have to think of something else." He raised his glass to her. "And she certainly did just that when she sold Weatherby House to you, and all your friends moved in."

Carla leaned back. Her mouth twitched. "Well, I can promise you I won't wade naked in any goldfish ponds."

"Ah, but can you speak for your friends?"

"I wouldn't presume to do so."

"That's what they're afraid of." He leaned forward slightly, his gaze moving caressingly over her face, lingering finally on her mouth. "Now that business is out of the way, let's talk about you."

Her defenses rose immediately. "What about me?"

"I want to know who Carla Gelsey is, where she came from, where she's been, and why she came back here."

"That's rather a lot for one evening."

"We'll have as many evenings as it takes."

Her mouth tightened. "All this to fulfill your sworn civic duty?"

The brown eyes glinted with sudden anger.

Tomaso arrived just in time and delivered the steaming herb-spiced pasta. Carla smiled gratefully at him. When he left, Blake leaned forward again.

"Let's clear something up," he said through his teeth. "I'm here with you for myself, not for anyone else."

"You led me to believe we were going to discuss Weatherby House and the latest problems that have arisen due to my purchase of it."

"We've done that. It was a good excuse to get you to come out with me, and it worked," he admitted without embarrassment. "If it hadn't, I'd have figured out another way."

"Should I be flattered?"

"Yes. I don't usually go to so much trouble."

Because he probably didn't have to, she thought bleakly. "Then why the effort this time?" she demanded, not wanting this interest.

"Because I'm more strongly attracted to you than any other woman I've ever met," he told her frankly, brown eyes clear. Carla's heart thudded. "Besides"— he smiled—"you obviously have brains and spirit. I

63

wanted to get to know you."

Every defense rushed to the fore. She lifted her chin and gave in to anger. "What you really mean is you'd like to take me to bed. My gray matter doesn't matter one damn bit."

His brows rose. He leaned back slowly and took a sip of wine. "Not immediately, but eventually I'd like to take you to bed, yes. Unless you're in a hurry, of course. I think I'd enjoy it very, very much. I think you would, too. It wasn't what I had planned for this evening, but if you—"

She started to stand, but he leaned forward and caught her wrist. With slight pressure he made her sit down again. "Would you rather I'd lied and said I found you attractive but all I'm interested in is a purely platonic relationship? I'm not."

"I'd rather you hadn't told me anything at all," she said shakily, wondering wildly if he could feel how fast her heart was going by the pulse in her wrist.

"Someone must have burned you pretty badly," he murmured, searching her face.

"You might say that," she whispered bitterly.

"Why don't you tell me about it?"

"Not likely." Rob Hanford was in her past, but he'd taught her a hard lesson about becoming involved with devastatingly handsome men.

"You look more angry than hurt," Blake observed. "I've a feeling it was your pride that took the real beating."

She sighed and tried to force herself to relax. "I don't

let myself dwell on it that much."

"No, you just let it fester and get in the way of any other meaningful relationship with a man."

"And you're offering me a *meaningful* relationship?" Again she tried to free herself. When she couldn't, she looked at him with quiet desperation. "Can we please talk about something else?"

He let her go slowly. "Anything you want, *except* Weatherby House."

Her wrist still tingled from his touch, and she put both hands beneath the table, well out of his reach. His eyes softened mockingly.

Tomaso appeared and looked down with disapproval. "You're not doing justice to my pasta! Leave the love talk for later and eat. Eat!"

Carla glanced at Blake and laughed. Tomaso stood beside the table, hands on his hips. "I'll come back in ten minutes and I want to see empty plates!"

Blake shrugged when he departed. "Tomaso takes his cooking seriously."

"So I see."

Between courses they talked. Much to her surprise, Carla found herself opening up to Blake's easy charm. Mostly, she spoke of her parents.

"Dad would build a house from the foundation up and Mom would decorate the inside and plan the gardens. As soon as everything was finished, they'd put it on the market, and when it sold we'd move on to another town. He always worked for himself."

"What'd your father build here in Allandale?"

65

She tented her fingers and smiled. "A little three-bedroom Tudor cottage at the end of Maple Street. I drove by it when I first came back. It looks much the same as it did when I lived there."

"A Tudor," Blake said thoughtfully.

"I suppose you'll say it's a bit out of place here," she said, looking at him in level challenge. "But it was one of my favorite homes. There was a patterned brick patio in back with a wisteria-covered arbor. I used to love to sit there in the spring." She drew her gaze forcibly away from his and looked instead at the burning candle on the table, letting the warm memories fill her. "By Easter it was like being inside a lavender cloud."

"Heady stuff, wisteria," Blake agreed, smiling slightly. "What else did your father build?"

She raised her eyes to meet his again and laughed softly. "In New Mexico it was a little adobe ranch house; in Colorado, a Swiss chalet. In Pennsylvania he built a red-and-white barn-style house with dormer windows on the second floor. Then in Maine Dad built a New England clapboard cottage. I think he tried everything except a grass hut and an igloo."

"How did you like moving around so much?"

"Sometimes I didn't like it at all. I'd no sooner make friends and feel part of things when we'd sell and move on again. For a while I hated the smell of sawdust, wood, and paint." She gazed into the candlelight reflectively. "But all in all, it was a special life. They were very special people."

"Your father never worked for anyone else?"

"No." She shook her head, glancing up. "My father was his own man. He didn't have a general contractor's license. In fact, he never apprenticed in carpentry or graduated from high school either. He was a self-taught man, and everything he ever built was the work of an artisan. His houses will stand longer than any of these tract homes they're building now."

Blake's mouth curved sardonically. "Are you voicing your father's prejudice or your own?"

"It's a shared prejudice," she said coolly.

"You don't think much of your own peers then, do you?" he asked, his eyes glinting.

She gave him a brilliant smile. "That depends on the peer, Mr. Mercer."

"Have you seen any of the homes or buildings I've designed and put up?" He refilled her wineglass.

"Frankly, the only piece of your work I've seen is the sketch you tacked up at the city council meeting. I wasn't impressed," she told him frankly.

"So I gathered." He grinned. "But that's a matter of taste, isn't it? You go in for gingerbread and dry rot."

She kept her smile. "There's very little dry rot at Weatherby House, as I'm sure you know."

He laughed softly and leaned forward. "How does your father feel about his daughter becoming a general contractor?"

The change of subject back to her father startled her. "Because my father lacked formal education doesn't mean he was prejudiced against it. He

67

encouraged me to go on to college."

Blake watched her face intently. "Why so defensive, Carla? I wasn't criticizing. I was only asking."

She said nothing for a long moment, turning her wineglass slowly. Blake Mercer threw her off balance. She didn't like the feeling. Even now she could feel him studying her closely, as though looking for something. What? Some weakness on which to play in order to win the battle over Weatherby House? Or was she too defensive, too quick to see subterfuge, too quick to grasp hurt and abandon trust?

Raising her head, she looked squarely at him. His dark brown eyes glowed with a sensual regard and interest she couldn't ignore. A tingling sensation grew in the pit of her stomach, swirling downward, and the fluttering in her chest became a hard, rapid pounding. Heartily resenting her own response to him, she turned her face away and stared out the window.

"You're not just defensive about your parents, are you?" Blake observed frankly. She turned back to give him the full force of her blue eyes.

"I've never really enjoyed being looked upon as a thick slice of prime rib, ready for the eating," she returned.

His brows rose slightly, eyes sparkling with laughter. "I'm that obvious? Sorry. I'll try to be a little more subtle about my attraction." He gave her a bland, innocent look. "Is this any better?"

"I've the feeling subtlety isn't one of your strong points."

"True." He smiled. "Nor is it one of yours, Miss Gelsey. If I've been looking at you like prime rib, you've been looking at me as though I were a platter of chopped liver."

She smiled, eyes dancing. "Dog food?"

"Dried and sacked," he agreed ruefully. "Tell me, how can I change your poor opinion of me?"

"Sell your share of Weatherby House," she returned bluntly.

His eyes narrowed, the good humor dissolving. "We agreed not to discuss business tonight."

"You asked, I answered." She shrugged.

"Lady, you've got a one-track mind."

"Let's say I'm very direct about what I want," she returned sharply.

"Oh, I can be very direct, too, when the occasion calls for it," he said, a smile playing at the corners of his mouth. "How direct an approach can you handle, Carla?"

Color suffused her face. "I suggest we change the subject. Again."

"I'm finding this topic infinitely titillating," he murmured, his gaze moving leisurely over her flushed face and downward to the quickening rise and fall of her full breasts. She felt as though he were physically touching her, and her fingers curled tightly in her lap.

"Well, *I'm* not," she said frankly.

"No? Well, since I'm having the greatest difficulty thinking of anything else of equal interest, perhaps you could make a suggestion?"

She leaned forward slowly, giving him a wide-eyed look of exaggerated interest. "Why don't you tell me all about yourself?"

"While you do what?" he drawled, chuckling.

"Oh, I'll listen with the raptest attention," she replied sweetly, resting her chin in the palm of her hand and fluttering her lashes.

His mouth tipped. "What do you want to know?"

She pretended surprise. "I didn't think it'd be necessary to probe. All a woman usually has to do is give a man a small opening and he'll pour out his life story."

He leaned back, mouth twitching. "You've been dating some real winners, haven't you?"

She kept her smile, sweetening it even more as she looked him over just as obviously as he had been staring at her. "Indeed. Now just begin with your birth, and I'm sure you'll have no problem going on and on from there."

He laughed softly.

"If it's dull, just spice it up with a few adventures—real or imagined—along the way," she added.

"You said at the council meeting I lacked imagination."

She spread her palms innocently. "A difference in taste." She hoped she didn't look as angry as she felt. Keeping her smile, she reached out and refilled his wineglass. "Perhaps your jaw needs a little lubrication."

"You're a very determined lady."

"You're just beginning to find that out?"

"I had an idea before." He smiled wryly. "You said

begin with my birth and go on and on." He raised his brows questioningly, then said: "I was born to wealthy parents. As soon as I was old enough, I went to boarding schools. From there I went on to Stanford for my undergraduate work and then to Columbia for my master's in architectural design. I needed a break, so I spent two years roaming around Europe before I came back to apprentice in New York. A firm in Los Angeles offered me a job, and after a few years there I came back to Sacramento to start my own business. Like your father, I preferred being my own man, my own boss. And like you, I had fond memories of Allandale—and summers with Aunt Mary. I bought a piece of land and built a house so I could weekend here. At the moment I spend my life running back and forth between Allandale and Sacramento." He spread his hands. "What else do you want to know?"

Carla found herself becoming interested, in spite of her fierce resolve to remain aloof. "Come now, you can do better than that, I'm sure. That's the bare bones, and you make it all sound like a job resumé. Where's the romance, the adventure?"

He gave her a level look. "Numerous encounters, little romance, and one marriage, brief and painfully enlightening."

Her lips parted slightly as she stared back at him. The expression in his eyes made her feel ashamed. Her defiance wilted. She sighed heavily and lowered her gaze from his. "I'm sorry. I don't usually behave so badly."

"Why the attack, Carla? Was I getting too close for comfort?"

Raising her head, she looked at him and decided that he really seemed interested. He was watching her intently, his face softened by something he found in hers. Worse than the way Blake Mercer was looking at her was the way he was making her feel. Suddenly she wanted to tell him everything, to pour out her life and hopes and hurts. Frightened by the impulse, she drew back, folded her napkin, and put it on the table.

"It's late. I think we should leave."

His mouth set. "I think we should stay right here and talk."

She glared at him. "I've said all I'm going to."

"Your hand is shaking."

She put her hand in her lap, and he gave her a questioning look.

Did Allandale even have taxis?

Blake seemed to read her mind. "There's no need to panic, Carla. I'll take you home," he said slowly. He signaled Tomaso for the bill.

They said nothing on the four-mile drive back to Allandale. When Blake pulled up to the curb, Carla unhooked the seatbelt. He caught her wrist. "Sit tight," he said, his eyes glittering angrily in the darkness.

"I'm quite capable of opening the door myself. I'm a big girl, Mr. Mercer."

"Then stop acting like a child," he rapped out, yanking his door open and getting out in a quick, agile motion that made his anger clear. She felt a wave of heat flood her face. He opened her door and grudgingly she took his extended hand and allowed him to help her from the low car. She was aware of him looking at her legs as she swung them around. Pulling her hand free, she lifted her chin.

"Thank you. I can see myself to the door."

"I'm an old-fashioned boy who likes to see his date safely in." He smiled tauntingly.

She opened the front gate with an angry swipe of her hand.

"Careful, you might break the rusty hinges off," Blake commented. "We need a flashlight. Cynthia Seder is right about this garden. A dozen muggers could hide here without being seen."

"If you're worried about it, why don't you go back to your car?"

He laughed softly. "Good try, Carla, but I'm going to see you to the front door whether you like it or not." He put his hand on her waist. "Now go slowly so you don't trip and break your neck." She could hear the laughter in his voice and wanted to move back on his instep. But she was more eager to get away from him.

Each step closer to the stairs, veranda, and front door quickened Carla's heart until it was racing nervously. Blake hadn't removed his hand from her waist, and its warmth was spreading through her. Her palms were sweating. Why was she so nervous?

When they reached the front door, she turned. "Thank you for dinner."

Blake grinned brutally down at her. "Are you planning to shake my hand?"

Hot color spread across her cheeks and down her neck. Her chin came up. "I wasn't planning to do anything." As she started to turn away, Blake's hand came up and flattened against the frame of the screen door, preventing her from opening it.

"No? Well, I was."

As she glanced up, startled, his mouth came down over hers in a heady kiss. His lips were firm and warm, and for a long moment that was all of him that touched her. Then one arm slipped slowly around her waist, drawing her away from the door. She put her hands up against his forearms, meaning to push him away, and found herself drawn even more closely against him as his hand left the doorframe to spread across her back, pressing her breasts against his chest. His hands moved down to arch her hips forward against his, and she became aware of the effect she was having on him.

He raised his head and nuzzled her neck. "Tell me now that I took you out to talk business," he said huskily.

Her breath came in sharp gasps. Her body felt scorched where it touched his, and rather than pushing him away as she'd intended, her fingers curled tightly onto his jacket sleeves, hanging on. She felt his warm lips move from the curve of her neck up along her jawline, seeking.

"No," she rasped. "That's enough," she told him, dismayed and embarrassed by the low timbre of her voice. She turned her head away when he started to kiss her again, but he merely moved gently against the other side of her neck, raising tingling goosebumps along her arching spine. His breathing was as uneven as hers.

"I'd say it wasn't half enough," he murmured softly. "Not nearly enough." His mouth covered hers again, and she felt the tip of his tongue run along the soft sensitive fullness of her upper lip.

"No." She put her hands flat against his chest and pushed back.

His arms relaxed, and he smiled slightly. He straightened away from her slowly, brushing his fingertips lightly against her flushed cheeks. She wondered vaguely if he could feel how hot they were.

"Lunch tomorrow?"

"No." Her refusal came out more sharply than she intended. He raised his brows faintly, laughter lighting his eyes.

"Dinner then?"

"No."

"You're not free," he drawled ruefully.

He was teasing her, and her tension and resentment grew. "I'm free. I'm just not interested in going out with you again and having a repeat performance of this."

He leaned against the door and gazed down at her, laughing softly, his eyes crinkling at the corners. "Come now, Carla, you can do better than that, I'm sure," he needled her with her own words. "Go out with me again," he said more softly.

"Once was more than enough."

"That's not the way the saying goes. I think we could

75

sort out our differences in a friendly way."

Carla knew just what he meant by a "friendly way," and she bristled at the suggestion. "I'd say the situation was perfectly clear right now."

His smile grew rueful, though his eyes danced. "I thought we were getting along admirably well for being in opposing camps." The light from inside the house showed enough of his face that she was aware of his gaze taking in the quick rise and fall of her sensitized breasts. "Very admirably," he added with a smile. "In fact, I've seldom found a business discussion quite so . . . arousing."

"Good night, Mr. Mercer," she snarled, turning away to yank the door open.

He laughed. "Sweet dreams, Miss Gelsey."

Chapter Six

When Carla came downstairs the following morning, she found Blake Mercer drinking coffee with Mary at the dining room table. Exquisite Havilland china cups and saucers were laid out as though she were entertaining the Prince of Wales. Blake glanced up and smiled faintly as Carla stopped in the doorway.

"Good morning, Miss Gelsey," he drawled and Mary looked up as well, a bright welcoming smile wrinkling her face.

"Sit down, dear, and join us." She waved her hand for Carla to come in.

Carla took a few steps into the room and hesitated. Blake's gaze was almost physical as he took in her snug jeans and loose, pale green T-shirt with its long sleeves and square neckline. She chose to ignore his disturbing presence and directed her attention to Mary, who was looking questioningly at the two of them.

"Have you eaten, Mary, or may I fix you something?"

She shook her head. "Oh, Blake's already taken very good care of me with one of his cheese omelets. I usually don't take breakfast, but he's such a grand chef I couldn't resist the temptation." She reached out to pat his hand affectionately. He grinned at her.

"Flattery will get you everywhere, Aunt Mary."

She chuckled. "Oh, I know dear. I learned that a long, long time ago."

Carla found herself staring at the open collar of Blake's cotton plaid shirt, which revealed tanned skin and dark swirls of hair. Her toes curled in her work boots, and she felt an unwelcome awareness in the pit of her stomach. It was a definite error in good judgment to be attracted to this man. What was the matter with her?

Forcing her eyes away from him, she smiled bleakly at Mary. "Well, then, if you'll excuse me . . ." she said, and retreated across the room and through the swinging door into the kitchen. Sighing with relief, she set about trying to find the cast-iron frying pan. She was bending down to check a cabinet beneath the counter when the kitchen door swung in again and she saw Blake's long denim-clad legs. She straightened abruptly and hit her head on a cabinet door that had been left open.

"Ouch!" She rubbed the spot with a wince and glared at Blake. "You surprised me."

"I'd ask if you were all right, but with a head as hard as yours, I'm sure you are. Did you do any damage to the door?"

"I was looking for the frying pan. Since you used it last, would you happen to know where it is?"

"It's in the sink. I haven't washed it yet."

"I'll do it." She turned away and snatched up the scouring pad on the washboard. Glancing back over her shoulder, she saw Blake standing with his arms crossed over his chest, his hip against the butcher block, watching her. "You're here awfully early, aren't you?" she said, glancing at her wristwatch. "It's only six-thirty."

"I know my aunt makes a habit of getting up around five-thirty, and there was something I wanted to discuss with her."

"More coercion?" Carla asked sweetly.

"Coercion only makes her dig her heels in further," he answered with a wry lift of his lips.

"Mercer charm then?"

"Not the same brand I tried on you last night, Miss Gelsey," he drawled, eyes glowing in amusement. She blushed and kept her face turned away from him while she put the frying pan on the gas range and went to the old round-fronted refrigerator, which was humming loudly in the corner. After taking out bacon and eggs, she walked back to the stove.

"Are you always this edgy in the morning? Or is it because you didn't sleep any better than I did last night?"

His tone brought her head up and around to look at him, and the expression of slumbering sensuality in his dark eyes brought fiery color into her cheeks. She hadn't slept well, and he had been the cause of her restlessness. That he should comment on it so openly made her defensive and angry.

"I didn't expect to find you here almost before dawn."

"You did turn me down for lunch and dinner."

He was laughing at her and her temper simmered. Slapping four strips of bacon into the pan, she turned on the gas.

"I suggest you strike your match first or you're liable to blow yourself up," he told her casually. "That's an old stove you're dealing with there, and it expects to be treated with proper respect."

She shut off the gas. "There were matches right here yesterday." She pointed.

"Look six inches to your right."

Gritting her teeth, she snatched up the box of matches and removed one. It took three strikes to get a light, and she could hear Blake chuckling softly from behind her. Her heart knocked angrily against her breastbone. As she turned the knob and lowered the match, there was a loud *whompf* and she jumped back with a gasp.

Blake straightened from the butcher block and leaned his elbow on the counter to the right of the range. "Did you singe your hair?"

She let her breath out slowly, ignoring him.

"Maybe you need a good cup of coffee to wake you up," he suggested, overly solicitous.

She twisted the knob and the flame shot high, licking hungrily around the bottom of the pan. Fat popped violently as the strips of meat sizzled, bubbled, and writhed. Carla tried to flatten them with a fork.

Blake straightened and came up behind her, looping one arm around her waist and drawing her back against him as his other hand reached past her to turn down the gas.

"You're burning your bacon, Miss Gelsey," he murmured, not releasing her. His breath was warm against her hair, and his fingers spread arousingly over her stomach. Worse, she could feel his body against her back. She wondered distractedly if he could feel her heart, which was pounding so hard she was sure she trembled with each beat.

"Will you please let go of me?" she rasped.

He didn't. "Just relax and calm down before you do yourself some harm. I'm not that threatening, am I?"

She closed her eyes tightly, her lips pressing together at the teasing huskiness of his voice. His hard biceps were warm against the curves of her breasts. How was she supposed to relax?

His arm loosened slowly from around her until she was free. But only for a moment. He rested both of his hands on her hips before stepping away entirely and leaning down on the counter again to assess the expression on her face. "Are you always self-destructive when you wake up?"

"If you came to visit with Mary, why are you in here bothering me?"

"Is that what I'm doing? Bothering you?" His mouth twitched.

She turned the bacon over, trying to ignore him, but that seemed impossible. His presence seemed to fill the room and cause an odd constriction in her chest, a tightening in her stomach. The way he was looking at her did nothing to help the situation either. He was attracted to her, and he was making no effort at all to hide the fact. The very smile he wore seemed a blatant advertisement.

Carla forked the strips of blackened bacon out of the pan and onto a paper towel. She cracked an egg into the grease and promptly broke the yoke. The second egg matched the first.

"Is this the way you usually cook?" Blake needled.

"I cook to eat. I've got better things to do with my time than create omelets."

He laughed. "Let's call a truce, Carla. I only came over this morning to take a tour of the house with you."

"What for?"

He was suddenly all business, his dark eyes direct and clear. "To see just what kind of project you're thinking of tackling. Once we go through the whole place and really take a look at what needs doing to renovate Weatherby House, I think you'll change your mind."

"Don't count on it."

He raised his hands in a surrendering gesture. "Just an intelligent discussion, that's all I'm asking."

She scraped her eggs onto a dish and put the pan in the sink, running water over it until the sharp hiss of cold against hot stopped. "I've got work to do in the basement."

"It won't hurt to leave it to your men for an hour. Besides, you ran out of lumber yesterday. You'll have to send one or both for more . . . if you have the funds."

She pushed through the swinging door, hoping it would catch him on its backward course. Mary had departed the dining room for her morning rocker ride on the veranda while she waited for the paper boy. Carla sat down and reached for the coffee pot.

Blake stood with his hands on the back of a Chippendale chair, his expression no longer amused. "All this anger because I kissed you last night?" he asked. "Aren't you being a little—"

"Last night has nothing to do with this morning!" she flared at him, slamming her fork down on the table.

"'Methinks the lady doth protest too much'," he quoted with an infuriating smile.

"And the lady thinks you've got one colossal ego. Jacque kisses better than you do."

He raised his brows. "I'd heard women were going for younger men these days, but isn't four a bit much?" he drawled. "Maybe I can do a better job of it next time, hmmm?"

She drew in a slow, calming breath of air. "Look, Mercer, I don't need you poking around Weatherby

House like a hungry termite in the foundations."

"Then you're admitting there are some." He grinned.

"You've got your own projects. Why don't you go tour them?"

"I've taken a day off to have a good look at yours," he countered, not the least discouraged.

"Well, it's not my day off. Come back a week from Saturday and I'll see if I can squeeze you into my schedule," she said, taking up her fork again. Blake pulled out the chair and sat down. She glanced at him after swallowing several bites of egg. The man was not going to take no for an answer.

"You don't need me to look around," she told him with a wide gesture. "You own ten percent of Weatherby House."

"I want you with me."

The way he looked at her when he said it made her heart start pounding again. She shrugged and forced herself to concentrate on her breakfast. It was very difficult with Blake lounging not six feet from her and watching every bite she took. She sipped her coffee, eyeing him warily over the rim of the cup. He gave her a slow, provocative smile.

"You've a hearty appetite, Miss Gelsey."

"I work hard," she replied.

"Two eggs, four strips of bacon, toast, coffee. You'd have to work hard to burn all that off." His eyes made an inventory of her assets. "It appears you do."

She gave him a stiff-lipped smile, knowing full well he was only trying to fluster her again. "Jogging helps," she remarked, looking him over as he had her and noting dismally that he had no spare fat either: Six-foot-three of hard-packed, well-formed male. He had the kind of body that would probably look magnificent spread across two pages of a women's magazine, modeling a swim suit, or just plain modeling.

"How many miles?"

"What?" She stared blankly at him.

"How many miles do you jog?" he repeated patiently.

"Three. Why? Do you run?"

"I'm sure I could keep up with you."

"I run by myself," she said firmly.

"Why? Afraid of a little competition?"

She set her cup and saucer on the empty breakfast plate and stood up. "It's been nice, Mercer, but I've got work to do."

"First, our tour," he said, straightening from the chair.

She sighed in exasperation. "You know very well you came to convince me that Weatherby House is not worth a rehab effort, rather than to be convinced it is. Spending an hour arguing is a waste of my time and yours."

"You might have missed something I didn't," he returned, looking as though it really mattered to him.

"Or you might have seen something that wasn't there," she retorted. "You've already made up your mind about this place."

The brown eyes blazed angrily and narrowed. "If you're so convinced that this is a viable project, I would think you'd be only too eager to point out my own incompetence. That is, unless you're already aware of your own."

She drew herself up to her full five-foot-seven, and glared at him. "You've got your grand tour, Mr. Mercer. Just give me a few minutes to rinse these dishes and leave instructions for Sam." She shouldered through the swinging door.

They started in the basement. Carla was still fuming and tense. Blake Mercer's back was rigid and his face set as he walked along the walls, pointing out evidence of dry rot and possible termite damage, accounting the rising cost of lumber and time needed to replace timbers. He had obviously come prepared to do battle. One wasted hour, she growled to herself, thinking of all the things she'd rather be doing than arguing with Blake Mercer. He'd bulldoze this house over her dead body!

"You've finished about half the work down here that's going to be necessary," he went on. "You ran out of lumber yesterday. Your estimate was optimistic at best." He made a wide gesture. "This is just the beginning. We haven't gone through a fraction of the house yet. Shall we?" His brown eyes were glinting as he warmed to his subject.

"In a minute, Mr. Mercer," she said and wove her way past power tools, sawhorses, damaged lumber still to be removed, and the old heating-system pipes that gave the basement a netherworld appearance.

"Congress estimated two million dollars to build the Sam Rayburn House Office Building," Blake went on, "and provided a safety-valve appropriation for whatever additional sums might be necessary. Those 'additional sums' came to eighty-eight million. Are you planning to make an astronomical error in your estimates as well, Miss Gelsey?"

"No. I think I can manage better than my male counterparts. Even you, Mr. Mercer. Your hotel complex in Seattle cost three million dollars more than you estimated."

His mouth flattened out. "You've been busy."

"Since you're so fond of quotes, here's one for you: 'Know your enemy.'" She made a sweeping gesture with her hand. "Look around again and you'll note that every one of the timbers you pointed out already has a chalk mark on it for removal or repair. I didn't miss one!"

She slapped her hand hard against a thick beam above her head. "This foundation was built from solid, seasoned redwood."

Blake turned, picked up a hammer, and put it between two wallboards. She saw his shirt stretch taut over his broad back and bulging biceps as he ripped outward. Half the board broke loose in his hands. Turning, he held it toward her. "Here's your solid, seasoned redwood, Carla. It's a wonder this place hasn't fallen down already."

She ground her teeth as she looked from his rigid face to the decayed board. She tapped her finger on a chalk mark near his right hand. "It was coming out anyway, as you can see. You saved me doing it myself. But I have to tell you, Blake, you do very messy work."

He tossed the board past her to crash and clatter over the others already discarded. He dusted off his hands before putting them on his hips. "Redwood is damnably expensive to replace, Carla. Can you afford it?"

"That's my problem, not yours."

"Weatherby House isn't your problem. It's Allandale's, and mine, and my Aunt Mary's. People aren't willing to stand around twiddling their thumbs while you do your experiment in preservation."

"This is no experiment. I've sunk everything I have into this. I believe in the project or I wouldn't have risked everything I own and a year and a half of my life to do it! Weatherby House was built by craftsmen with quality materials, Mercer. It isn't one of your modern potboilers thrown up and held together by spit and sheetrock. It's worth preserving!"

He watched her face closely and then said very calmly, "Shall we continue the tour in the kitchen?"

She waved her hand toward the stairs. "Be my guest."

Once upstairs, Blake pointed out the cracked ceiling and wall plaster, the buckled and split linoleum, the mildewed caulking between the counter tiles, the loose doorframe, rusty pipes, and ancient wiring.

Carla let his dismal diatribe pour over her while she viewed everything through her own visions of how the room would look after restoration. She walked across the cracked, faded floor and ran a loving hand over the tiled counter. Blake stopped speaking and watched her.

She smiled. "Look at how this was built, Blake. No particle board here. No fiberglass. Not even a cheap nickel nail. No machine-made tile." She traced a pattern on one of the larger tiles set among the many smaller pale yellow ones. "These tiles aren't even made anymore. They used to do them in Southern California, but now no one bothers. No one has the patience or willingness for it. No one has the skill. It's been lost." She looked up and across at him, where he stood with his hand resting on the butcher block, a curious look on his face that she didn't want to decipher.

"The only other places I can remember seeing this kind of tile were at Zane Grey's house on Catalina Island, and at San Simeon."

"Salvage them," Blake reasoned. "I haven't claimed there weren't things of value in Weatherby House. Every door in this place is solid oak."

A touch of laughter lit her blue eyes. "I didn't think you'd noticed."

His gaze moved intently over her face, taking in each feature. The grimness left his dark eyes and a faint smile lit them. "Believe it or not, I know the difference even through twenty or more layers of enamel paint. There's a certain ring to the wood."

"Good—there may be hope for you after all," she replied smoothly.

Their gazes met and held. Carla could feel her breath catch in her throat as she saw his hard, cold eyes become velvety. With an effort she drew her gaze away and looked around, trying to focus her thoughts onto their discussion and away from the unwanted attraction she felt for this man.

"Everything you mentioned is cosmetic," she told him.

"The back doorframe isn't square. That usually means a structural problem."

"I noticed it. It has to do with the beam below us. We need to jack it up another few centimeters. No big problem." She waved her hand airily. "Now, as I was saying, the caulking, plastering, new linoleum—"

"Where are you going to get this kind of linoleum? Or are you planning to put in the no-wax vinyl stuff?"

She grinned. "I wouldn't be so sacrilegious. There are sources. There's one company back in a little town in Tennessee that still makes just this kind of linoleum. In fact, they even have a pattern very much like this one with a wide yellow strip around the outside and the marbling effect of whites, brown, and yellows in the middle. It's quite attractive." She turned as she continued, growing more excited with her plans.

"We'll strip the cabinets back to bare wood and restain them the natural wood tones. The fixtures and handles will have to be cleaned, but look at them." She knelt down and picked at one paint-covered knob on a lower cabinet door. "Brass."

Straightening, she turned toward him. "Come on, I want to show you some other treasures of Weatherby House."

Pushing through the swinging door, she entered the dining room again. "This built-in china cabinet is mahogany. See the grain. Feel it. It's almost as though it's still alive and warm. And look at the beveled-glass windows up here, and these crystal knobs on all the drawers." Stepping away, she used her foot to push back the worn rug. "Wood floors."

"In pretty bad shape," Blake commented.

"With proper sanding, restaining, and verathane, they'll be like new."

"Carla, you can't use disc sanders on this kind of thing. You're talking about hand work, hours and hours of hand work."

"Who mentioned anything about disc sanders?" She marched through the archway into the big front parlor. "You can't see it, but there's stained glass all along the top panes of these big picture windows over here." She pulled back the faded and worn brocade drapes and began to cough at the dust that clouded around her.

Blake laughed. "Quite a dust trap."

She didn't look at him but heard him walk toward the fireplace. Carla sneezed violently as she struggled to escape the folds of material.

Blake waited, then grinned at her as she appeared, pushing her hair back from her flushed face.

"This fireplace," he said, pointing. "It's badly clogged with pine pitch." Running an expert hand along the seam against the wall, he added grimly over his shoulder, "And the masonry is breaking away on this side." He stepped back, looking for more bad news. Pulling the heavy drapes all the way to one side, he was gratified with more findings. "These windows are painted shut and the hardware is broken." He kicked the wall lightly. "The sideboards along this wall are badly decayed, which means there's more than likely additional damage inside the wall in the studs and frame." He stopped and put his hands on his hips. "Ah, what have we here?" he drawled in amusement. "It seems you have guests already."

Carla pulled back Mary's chair to see what he was talking about. A big rat hole was chewed in the baseboard. "A little poison will take care of them."

"From the size of the hole, I think you'd better invest in a bazooka." Blake commented dryly, watching her pale face.

"A few rats aren't going to run me out of this house. You"—she sneezed again—"included!"

He laughed softly while she searched her pockets for a handkerchief.

Walking around the chair so that he stood right in front of her, he casually took his own handkerchief from his back pocket and held it out for her with a mocking smile. "It seems the lady preservationist has an allergy to dust."

He was so close, she could feel the heat of his body and smell the scent of his musk and wood aftershave. Heady stuff, she thought, heart pounding. She sniffed indignantly, resenting his effect on her, and debated using the back of her own sleeve to solve the dilemma rather than accept the monogrammed linen he dangled in front of her nose. Necessity won out.

"Thank you," she said haughtily, taking the handkerchief and spreading it out. Lifting her head, she raised her brows at him. "Ironed?" she drawled.

"My housekeeper insists on spoiling me." He chuckled.

"Well, don't expect to get it back the same way," she told him firmly, just managing to cover a sneeze that rocked her back on her heels.

He grinned. "After seeing the way you cook, I was fairly sure you didn't iron."

She blew her nose before giving him a sweet if watery smile. "I'll wash it and return it," she said, pushing it into her back pocket.

"No hurry. I have one or two others."

She walked out into the foyer. "Since you're familiar with the study and your aunt's rooms, we'll skip those, unless you insist," she said in flat, businesslike tones. She put her foot on the lower step and glanced back at him as he stood leaning against the parlor doorjamb, watching her with a smile that bordered on a smirk. "Shall we go upstairs and have a look at the bed-rooms?"

His grin was broad and roguish. "Best offer I've had all morning." Straightening, he nodded toward the stairs. "After you, Lady Gelsey."

She was acutely aware of him behind her, and one backward glance confirmed her suspicions that his gaze was locked on her slender derriere. Blushing and gritting her teeth, she continued with dignity up the stairs and waited at the top as he followed at a more leisurely pace. He stopped just before the last step and looked with disconcerting directness into her rigid face. There was an amused curve to his mouth and a provocative gleam in his brown eyes.

Crossing his arms, he put his foot on the landing and leaned back casually against the balustrade while he continued to look her over. "You know, Miss Gelsey, there are certain things in this house which are very nicely put together."

She had the urge to plant her booted foot in the center of this broad chest and push. He would bounce well down the stairs, she was sure, but then he might do some damage to the woodwork.

"Is that so?"

He smiled slowly, and Carla felt an unwelcome sensation flare in the pit of her stomach and spread like fire up to her chest and out into her limbs.

"Good angles and curves. Quality construction."

She had run into this kind of sexual innuendo before and had never let it bother her. In fact, she'd often turned it around and made the man feel embarrassed. But Blake Mercer got under her skin. It was easy to play the game when she didn't feel anything; but when this man looked at her, he made her toes curl tightly in her boots. Even Rob Hanford hadn't affected her that way.

She put her hands on her hips. "Is this the way you usually conduct business?" she asked bluntly.

"Do you always rile so easily?" he countered.

"I like to be taken seriously."

"It was your idea to come up and look at the bedrooms."

"Well, we can always put off the tour if you don't

think you can handle it."

He laughed easily, apparently tiring of his game. "All right. Lead on, lady contractor," he said. "I'll do my best to concentrate."

Michelle and Jacque had gone downstairs to eat breakfast. The same with the men on the second floor. There were several problems in their rooms that Blake was only too quick to point out, but they were things Carla had already noted. He just had a way of making them sound worse.

Two other bedrooms were unused, the furnishings protected by dust-covers. They shared an ancient bathroom that boasted a claw-footed tub and a pedestal sink.

As they came up the last stairs and down the hall of the third floor, Carla passed her own bedroom door. "What about this one?" Blake asked, putting his hand on the crystal knob.

She didn't want him poking around in there. "It's just like the others. Let's go on down here and have a look at—"

Blake opened the bedroom door and walked in.

"Blake!" she protested and stormed in after him. He stood in the middle of her bedroom, looking around with interest. He took in the mattress and her down sleeping bag, and the fact that the rest of her things were stacked neatly in one corner. He also noticed she had stripped the room of all other furnishings, making it more of a work area than a place to live.

"Good lord," he muttered, letting his expert eye take

in each dismal detail. "This room is a disaster."

It was, she knew. That was why she had taken it for herself. It was the greatest challenge. She took in the cracked walls, the crumbling ceiling plaster, the warped floorboards outside the bathroom, the deteriorating fireplace. She could well imagine what Blake was thinking.

He turned and glared at her. "You're living in this?"

She hooked her thumbs in her pockets. "It can be restored."

"Why didn't you take one of those other bedrooms across the hall, or on the second floor? Why this one? It's the worst in the house!"

"That's precisely why I chose it. It needs the most work," she said, squaring her shoulders. The dark eyes narrowed. He shook his head in disgust.

"You're an idiot, Carla."

"Coming from you, I'll take that as a compliment," she retorted. "Now shall we get on with it? You did say you wanted to see the perimeter, didn't you?"

"Not so fast. We haven't been up to the attic yet."

She groaned inwardly, having hoped to bypass that. He knew the way, probably having been there before. There was a door between the two south bedrooms that opened into a narrow, dark stairway up to the attic. Flashlight in hand, Blake went first. With a sigh, Carla followed.

Extensive work would be needed up here, she knew, and this part of the project would be the most expensive. The beam of light in Blake's hand showed the warped, decaying floor of an enormous room that had once been used for grand balls. Now crates were stacked everywhere, and the place was eerily criss-crossed by spider webs. She heard a scurrying sound and tried to ignore it. There was a heavy, musty smell of rotting wood, and a draft came from somewhere off to the right. More bad news. Several narrow spears of light pierced the darkness. Blake noticed them immediately and gave her a look that made her bite down on her lower lip. He flashed the beam of light on the floor and showed the water damage.

"You need a new roof."

"I know," she admitted flatly, letting out a slow sigh.

"In fact," he said, looking around slowly again, "I'd say it's more accurate to say that you need a new top floor."

"Not quite, but you're close." She gave him a faint smile.

"How much, Carla?"

He was on the step above her and she had to tilt her head back to meet his steady, grim gaze. The planes of his handsome face were made sharper by the odd light, and his eyes seemed to glitter. "How much?" he repeated.

"Plenty."

"A dollar amount. I'm just curious to know how far off you are on this part of the project."

Her mouth tightened. "All right. Thirty-five thousand."

He gave a sharp laugh. "Closer to fifty. Maybe more."

"Possibly," she agreed sharply. "But my estimate will

still put me closer than yours did in Seattle!" She jerked around and marched down the stairs. She regretted ever having agreed to this tour.

Blake slammed the door behind him and strode back down the hallway to her bedroom. He tossed the flashlight on her down bag, gave one last disgusted look around the room, then slammed that door as well. "Shall we have a look at the exterior now?"

"Anything you say," she retorted, following him.

Of course he pointed out the problems with the gingerbread across the top of the veranda, around the windows, and along the eaves. Carla kept her face placid while inwardly she seethed.

"How you do love being a harbinger of gloom, Mercer!" she said finally, when he commented on the cost of painting the outside of the house.

"I don't look at things the way I want them to be but at the way they are," he told her angrily. "I'm not a dreamer; I'm a businessman."

She was breathing hard, holding her temper with difficulty. She smiled through stiff lips. "Good day, Mr. Mercer. I hope you enjoyed your tour." She started to walk away, but Blake caught hold of her arm and jerked her back.

His face was pale and rigid. "The roof, the top floor, and the basement should cost well over fifty thousand dollars."

"Don't worry about it, Mercer. If I run out of money, I'll get financing."

He let out his breath in exasperation. "Fat chance."

She yanked her arm free, but he caught hold of her shoulders to prevent her from stalking away. "Nobody in his right mind would pour money down a rat hole!"

She tried to shove his hands away, but his fingers tightened inexorably. As he searched her face, his own softened. "Why is this house so important to you?" he asked quietly. "There are others, Carla. Better ones. Give this one up. You'll wipe yourself out, and it'll still end up coming down."

She shoved his hands away. "My parents had hoped to return to Allandale and retire here. They never forgot this place. Dad admired this house. He said he always dreamed of being a part of building a great house like Weatherby. He never had the money, and he never had the education. This is the house that made me want to be an architect and general contractor! *This* house! Not some damn geometric structure made of steel and glass. *This!* I have the training, and Mom and Dad willed me everything they worked a lifetime to earn. Weatherby House stands, Mr. Mercer. She's going to stand for me and my Mom and Dad and anyone else who wants a beautiful piece of the past. It will be worth every penny of my inheritance to renovate her!"

His face softened further. "You've let it become too personal."

"You're damn right!"

"Carla, you can't do it," he told her gently.

"You just watch me!" She swung around and stalked away, too angry to let him see the sheen of tears in her eyes.

Chapter Seven

They finished the basement renovation three weeks later, but it put a sizable dent in Carla's assets. Blake reappeared several times a week, looking around and leaving after a brief visit with his great-aunt. Carla didn't speak to him, or acknowledge his presence, though she felt it every time he was there.

Since the work within the body of the house could wait, she next tackled the top floor and roof. She estimated it would take four months to complete this portion of the project. Soon after that the rainy season would begin.

First she called in an exterminator. Win Marshall was in his mid-forties, with crew-cut gray hair, sharp hazel eyes, a thin face and body. After a look around, he announced his dire conclusion: "The whole place should be tented."

She groaned inwardly, calculating the cost. "Just the top floor for now."

"Lady," he said patiently, mouth thinning, "you've got termites, silverfish, ants, black widow spiders, mice, rats, *and* bats."

"Yes," she said calmly, "I know. Just the top floor for now, please."

"Glad I'm not living here," he muttered.

With an extension ladder, hook, and ropes, Carla got herself up on the gabled roof for a better look around. Scaffolding would be put up shortly. For added safety, she wore cleated shoes and a harness.

From the highest peak, with one foot planted on either side of the steep pitch, she could see the whole length of Main Street, as well as the surrounding countryside. Below and around her the garden looked like a veritable jungle.

Marvin's head appeared at the edge of the roof as he made his way up. "Gees," he puffed. "I always swear I'll never do this again." His forearms bulged as he dragged himself up further, then came to his knees. "I hate heights."

"You've never told me that before," Carla teased. Marvin said it every time he climbed onto a roof.

He looked up at her dismally. "What're you playing at, Carla? King of the Mountain?"

"The view is great from up here." She saw some people gathering across the street in front of a shop to watch. She waved. No one waved back. Planning a lynching probably. She sighed inwardly and looked down. She wasn't exactly fond of heights herself, but it was all part of her trade.

"Just tell me about it," Marvin muttered and worked his way slowly across the steep gable.

Sam, Michelle, and Mary were standing on the dandelion-dotted lawn below, craning their necks to watch.

"How's it look up there?" Sam hollered through cupped hands.

"You want the truth or a fairy tale?" Marvin shouted back down.

Carla grinned at him. "It's not that bad." She looked around at the composition roof.

"Bad enough. Gees, have we got our work cut out for us up here. How do I get out of this outfit, anyway?"

Carla perched herself securely, pulled out her hammer, and began prying up nails and removing shingles. She tore back the tar paper to get a look at what was beneath.

"Look at these beauties!" she cried, finding scalloped wood shingles underneath.

"These are going to cost a bundle to replace," Marvin grunted, working on his own gable.

"With the right materials we can make them ourselves."

His head came up and turned slowly, taking in the size of the roof. "You've got to be kidding! How many thousands do you figure you can make in any one lifetime?"

Carla laughed easily. "I'll raise your salary—we'll add donuts to the breakfast menu."

"Make it bearclaws and we'll talk about it," he muttered, inching his way cautiously across the peaked roof and crouching gingerly on another gable.

Glancing down at Main Street, she saw a familiar green Jaguar approaching from the north end of town. Her attention sharpened on it. As it pulled up in front of Weatherby House, she resented heartily the way her pulse raced.

Looking down, she concentrated again on prying up the composition shingles and getting under the tar paper. Yet her eyes were drawn to the walkway, watching for Blake. When she saw him, her brows rose faintly, taking in his elegantly tailored three-piece gray business suit. Few men could wear one without looking thick-waisted and heavy. Blake looked magnificent, every inch the successful entrepreneur.

How long had it been since he'd been on a roof prying up shingles, she wondered, smiling to herself.

While she worked, she glanced at him. He walked leisurely toward his aunt, who stood on the lawn looking upward. Smiling a greeting, he glanced up to see what she was watching. Carla saw him stiffen as though rigor mortis had just set in.

"What in hell are you doing up there?" he hollered.

Carla glanced at Marv and rolled her eyes heavenward. Then she looked down at Blake and smiled sweetly. "What's it look like we're doing? Getting a suntan, of course."

Marv chuckled. "You're going to make the man mad, Carrie."

"Get down!" Blake shouted, the hands on his hips pushing back the flaps of his neat jacket.

"No need to worry. We're insured," she called down.

"Are we?" Marv asked with a grin.

"You wouldn't want to fall and find out, would you?" she teased.

Marv pulled on his rope and grinned. "Safe and secure."

Blake stood below, his face pale in anger. "Get down from there or I'll come up and drag you down!"

Carla straightened until she was standing fully upright, one foot planted on either side of the steepest peak on Weatherby House, the iron weather vane to her left. She spread her arms and grinned down at him tauntingly. "You'd be out of place up here in your business suit, don't you think?" she called down. She sat again and resumed working.

She tore back another layer of composition shingles and tar paper under the claw end of her hammer. "Eureka!" she cried, finding what she had hoped would be there. She pried up the nail with a squeak of old metal against wood and lifted another scalloped wooden shingle. "Look at this beauty!"

"I think he's coming up," Marv told her grimly.

"What?" Shocked, Carla turned and looked down again. Sure enough, Blake had stripped off his jacket and tossed it heedlessly to the grass. Next came his vest and tie. Then he was striding toward the side of the house where the ladder and ropes were positioned.

"He's coming all right," Marv nodded with certainty.

"In wing tips? He's not crazy!"

"He's mad, and he's coming. I just heard him swear."

"Tell him to get down, Marv."

"*You* tell him."

She lifted her head and hollered. "Get down, Mercer, before you break your stupid neck!"

"You coming down?"

"We're on our way!" She glanced at Marv. Giving an exaggerated sigh, she shrugged and said, "Go on down."

Marv lifted another fancy wooden shingle, gave her a broad wink, and tucked it in the big thigh pocket of his frayed desert pants. She made an airy gesture with her hand. "Gentlemen first."

Marv grinned. "Thank goodness for women's liberation." He made his way cautiously back to the roof edge. "See you below, Captain," he said and lowered himself away.

Carla tucked her shingle into the front of her workshirt. She dropped her hammer back into her carpenter's belt and then made her way carefully down the steep incline of the roof. Repositioning the rope at her waist and snapping the metal ring on it, she leaned far back and made a smooth mountain-climbing drop all the way to the ground, landing softly on her feet. Marv was still on the ladder.

"Slowpoke," she teased, unclipping her rope and stepping back. She turned and came up against Blake's broad chest. Gasping, she stepped back. His blue shirt was damp with perspiration and she could see the tanned skin and dark hair beneath. The musky male scent of his body went straight to her head. Her heart jumped crazily, little fingers of excitement stroking her nerves.

"Oh, hello," she said sweetly, raising her head slowly and seeing the dangerous glitter in his brown eyes. His face was very red and very taut.

Rage or exertion, she wondered, thinking of his climb up the ladder and partway up the rope.

His hands were on his narrow hips, his legs spread

and planted firmly. "You're out of your mind, you know that?" he said.

Rage, she decided. She pulled off her leather work gloves and spread her hands. "As you can see, there's not a scratch on me."

Raising her head, she saw that his anger had partially dissolved. He was staring with interest at the front of her shirt.

"What're you wearing? A new type of female foundation?"

Blushing, she extracted the shingle with as much dignity as possible. His mouth curved, and his stance became indolent.

"It's a beauty, isn't it?" she said brightly, turning it over in her hand and avoiding his steely glare.

"If you've got a thing for rotten old shingles."

She raised her head defiantly. "Doesn't everyone?" Stepping around him, she headed across the lawn toward Mary. Michelle and Sam were talking to Marvin.

Blake caught hold of her arm, pulling her back around to face him again. "You might have been killed."

"Did anyone ever tell you you're beautiful when you're angry?" she parodied the old male line.

His expression was satisfyingly comic, and she took the chance to extract her arm from his tight grip and further explain herself. "I needed to have a look around. We were perfectly safe. Don't sweat it."

Mary approached with her cane. "Carrie, you were

absolutely magnificent. What a thrill my old heart got when you came down off the roof like that!"

"What you mean is you damn near had a stroke," Blake muttered. "And don't encourage her, Aunt Mary. She's irresponsible enough as it is." He turned to Carla again. "You were perched up there like a weather-vane rooster," he snapped.

"A hen at least, dear," Mary put in, watching their argument with a faint smile.

"I've had some gymnastics training," Carla said flippantly. "I used to be quite good on the balance beam."

"Terrific," he drawled.

"It reminded me of a Tarzan movie," Mary chimed in brightly. "Especially when Blake started up the ladder to save you."

He gave her a warning glare. Mary's wrinkles deepened as she grinned at him unrepentantly. "Got your blood going, didn't it, dear?"

Carla lowered her head and laughed softly.

"She did remind me a little of Cheeta when she came off the roof," he agreed, relaxing.

Carla looked up at him and laughed openly. His color was returning to normal and the tightness around his marvelous mouth was relaxing. "Surprised you, did I?" she teased, raising her eyebrows up and down.

"Somewhat," he agreed, his mouth curving. He studied her face intently, eyes caressing each feature. The look gave her a sensual message that made her stomach flutter and her breath catch. She glanced at Mary and received a wink.

Trying to keep her tone light, she looked up at Blake again. "Well, now that you know I can swing myself down from high places, you won't have to panic." Clutching the old shingle, she headed across to Sam, Michelle, and Marv.

"Has he cooled down?" Michelle asked in a stage whisper.

Carla shrugged. Glancing back, she saw Blake was watching her with a faint smile on his face. Mary was saying something to him with a teasing grin. He nodded and smiled wider. Something about their exchange was making her decidedly nervous. She had the distinct feeling Blake Mercer was hatching some plan and Mary Weatherby was approving.

"Now that we have the pattern, we can begin manufacturing the shingles," she told her workers.

Sam groaned. "Look at that thing. It's darn near the shape of a heart."

"How many do you think we need?" Michelle asked, taking the shingle and turning it over in her hand.

Marv rolled his eyes. "Plenty."

"It's make them or buy them," Carla said dismally. "Frankly, I can't afford to buy them. I'm not even sure I could find a place that makes them. But we can get the wood, and I've got the jigsaw."

"Dream, dream, dream," Sam began singing, his tenor voice rolling out, blue eyes twinkling.

"Why not enlarge them?" Michelle suggested. "Make them twice this size. Then we won't need so many."

"Great idea. That'll save time and money."

Carla looked up at the great old house. "You know, it must have looked like a candy palace at one time. Something out of a Hansel and Gretel story."

"A three-layer cake," Sam agreed. "With fancy frosting. Who's going to paint the joint?"

Marv groaned theatrically and gave Carla a wicked side-long glance. "Caviar for appetizers. Champagne for brunch."

She laughed in good humor, but she was beginning to feel the immensity of the project she had undertaken. Dreams came at a high price. Before the house could be painted, it would have to be sanded down to the wood beneath the layers of peeling paint. Then it needed a primer coat before the two outer coats. How many colors for the gingerbread and at what cost? How many hours? How many days? How many weeks? More likely months.

But first they needed a new roof.

"Well, we aren't going to make any progress standing around here jawing," Sam commented with a heavy sigh. "I'll hit the lumber yard."

"I'll go with you," Marv offered. "After lunch," he added.

Carla gave him a playful punch in the arm. "How can anyone so skinny eat so much?"

He posed and flexed his muscles. "I'm a lean, mean machine."

Turning around toward the veranda, Carla saw Blake approaching. Her heart jumped. He nodded to the others as they passed, then came to a stop right in front of her. His closeness was almost overwhelming. He had his jacket and vest draped over his shoulder and the smile he wore made her cheeks heat.

"Did you have something to say?" she asked pointedly, looking straight up at him with her placid businesswoman's expression.

He searched her face, his own becoming solemn and intent. "You look a little down."

"Is that what you're hoping for?"

"Would anything I have to say at this point make any difference?" he asked, eyes hooded and watchful.

Her chin tipped. "Probably not."

He looked amused. "That's what I was afraid of." He smiled openly. Without taking a step, he seemed closer. His eyes darkened, and his expression softened. "Come out to dinner with me again, Carrie," he said softly.

His look made her feel warm all over, and her hostility seemed to be dissolving under the heated gaze which took in each feature of her face, lingering on her mouth. A wave of unwanted feelings surged up and spread.

"Come on," he said in a coaxing, husky tone, those firm yet sensually curved lips giving her a slow smile that made her swallow hard.

She cleared her throat softly. "No, I don't think so."

His brows lifted, challenging her. "No?"

"No." This time she spoke clearly, firmly.

He shrugged. She felt unreasonably disappointed that he was giving up so easily and then mentally shook herself. She glanced up at him sharply and saw he was still smiling, secret laughter shining in the brown depths of his eyes. She gave him a suspicious look.

"Was there something else?"

"Not at the moment."

"Were you coming in to visit with Mary?" She frowned faintly, hearing the half-hope in her tone.

He grinned. "In a few minutes. I have to get something out of my car first." He turned and sauntered back across the lawn toward the brick walkway. She watched him uneasily, sensing he was up to something and afraid to find out what. She went into the house and found everyone congregated around the dining room table, digging in to bologna-and-cheese sandwiches and tall glasses of milk. Mary glanced up.

"Where's Blake?" she asked, looking questioningly past Carla. "He said he was staying."

"He'll be in shortly. He had to get something from his car first."

"Oh, yes," she said brightly. "How could I possibly forget about that?" She laughed. "I've been after Blake for years about it, but he's never had the inclination, and he's always had a thousand excuses. I wonder what changed his mind?" She looked straight at Carla and gave her sweet urchinlike grin.

Carla frowned uneasily, having no idea what Mary was talking about. She was becoming decidedly nervous. "After him to do what, Mary?" she asked, preparing herself for a surprise. If there was anything she had learned about Mary over the past weeks, it was that she did, indeed, love stirring up a brew.

Sam cleared his throat and nodded to Carla to look

around. She saw Michelle and Marv staring past her, just as she heard something heavy drop on the floor behind her.

"To move in," Blake answered for his great-aunt as Carla swung around and saw the two large leather suitcases resting on either side of his powerful long legs. Arms akimbo, he smiled in malicious satisfaction as her face blanched.

"To what?" she gasped. "You can't!"

"I'm going to be a guest of your guest house," he told her easily.

"That's right," Mary confirmed brightly. "And about time."

"We're not open for business yet," Carla snapped at Blake. She looked back at Mary pleadingly. "Mary, he'll make trouble." *That* was a mistake.

Mary's eyes brightened noticeably. She waved her elegant withered hand airily. "Nothing you can't handle, dear." She smiled at her great-nephew. "Maybe you can put him to work, too. He's quite handy with tools, you know."

Carla groaned inwardly before turning back to Blake. "Now look, let's be . . ." she began, her voice trembling with agitation.

"Reasonable?" He smiled. "We tried that once before and ended without getting as far as I intended."

She blushed hotly, her mouth tightening in fury.

"This time," he said, "I'm going to go with a frontal attack, no holds barred."

His decidedly warm dark gaze swept her from

111

flushed face to heaving breasts and back again. Her heart was thundering.

"Hey, Blake," Sam said, laughter in his voice, "are you talking about the house?"

Blake gave them all a broad, bawdy grin and a wink that reminded Carla of his great-aunt. "That, too," he answered easily.

"Excuse me," Carla said tightly, not able to manage any more at that moment. She started to storm past him into the hallway, but he caught her easily about the waist and brought her up firmly against his side. He leaned down, and his lips were almost against her ear.

"Looks like we'll be having dinner together this evening, after all," he whispered, his warm breath raising goosebumps on her skin before he allowed her hasty retreat.

Chapter Eight

Carla spent the afternoon working in her bedroom, letting loose her frustration and temper on the plaster and boards that needed to be removed. They could probably hear her from downstairs as she used hammer and crowbar with scarcely suppressed fury. Luckily she had already moved her things to the small guest bedroom directly across the hall, for within half an hour her old room was as heavy with plaster dust as it was with muttered expletives.

It was nearly dusk when she decided to quit. Brushing

herself off, she went across the hall, gathered a few belongings, then headed for the only other functional bathroom on the second floor. She bypassed the big bedroom that had a spider condominium in the ancient private bath, and went into the one at the end of the hall to the right.

She showered at length. Dressed in a pair of lacy bikini panties, she dried her hair leisurely before the cracked mirror, then put on a light touch of makeup. Sitting on the carved oak toilet-seat cover, she pulled on her sheer pantyhose, strapped on her high-heeled metallic evening sandals, and stepped into a lacy half-slip. The simple burgundy silk dress hung on a hanger on a brass hook at the back of the dingy yellow enameled bathroom door. She slipped it over her head, letting the light, cool fabric shimmer down smoothly over her slender body. Finally she hooked the bronzed rose belt that accentuated her small waist. The skirt hung straight, a slit up one side revealing part of her shapely thigh. Gathering her toiletries, she stuffed them back into the canvas tote bag and opened the door.

Blake was leaning against the hall wall, arms crossed. If he had looked devastating in his three-piece business suit, he was even more disturbing in tight, faded jeans and a plaid workshirt, wide leather and construction boots.

Carla's mouth tightened in mutiny against the sensation he aroused just by standing there. She felt his gaze like a physical touch as it moved from the soft, thick hair flowing around her shoulders and down her back, to the full, firm swell of her breasts beneath the clinging silk, which made it embarrassingly clear she wore no bra, down to her slim hips and on to her silk-clad legs. And then up again.

His smile sent tingles along her spine. "Well, you do believe in dressing for dinner, don't you?"

"When I go out," she said pointedly, trying to give the appearance of perfect control while wondering if he could see just how angry he was making her. Her gritted teeth and heightened breathing gave her away.

His eyes narrowed. "Out?" He straightened from his indolent stance and walked slowly toward her. Each step he took increased the already racing tempo of her heart.

"Yes, out." She certainly wasn't going to stay here while he smirked and leered at her from across the dining room table.

"You should've told me you'd changed your mind and I'd have been ready. As it is, you're going to have to wait a few minutes."

Her eyes glinted as she gave him a cloying smile. "Never take anything for granted, Mr. Mercer, especially with a woman."

There was no mistaking the banked fire in his brown eyes. "You're going out alone—like that?"

"What's wrong with this?" she returned hotly.

"Nothing, as long as you've got a bodyguard along to keep men from touching what they can see." His eyes dropped to her breasts and lingered there. "Otherwise, you're asking for trouble."

"This isn't exactly see-through gauze, you know!"

"Not see-through, but clearly outlined. I hope you don't run into anyone with high blood pressure. You'd stand trial for manslaughter."

"Good night, Mr. Mercer."

He didn't stop her. It wasn't necessary. As she turned, she spotted a big pile of dirty dust-covers outside the big bedroom door. She froze. "What's this?" she demanded, pointing.

"What's it look like?"

She stood in the doorway and saw that the room had been swept, windows opened to air the place, and Blake's two suitcases were open on top of the old canopy bed still bare of sheets, blanket, and bedspread.

She turned and stared at him and gasped. "You're not moving in up here!"

"Why not?" He watched her with a decidedly roguish gleam in his eyes.

"Everyone else is on the second floor," she told him stiffly.

"You're up here."

"Precisely why I don't want you in there."

"Where's the problem?" he asked too easily. "I'm moving into the bedroom down the hall from you, not in with you."

That was just the point. Her new room opened into his.

"From the sounds of your working in there this afternoon, I thought you might have had a change of heart and decided to tear the house down after all." He nodded toward her old room.

"You can't move into *that* room," she said firmly.

"It's too late. I've moved in already."

"Well, you can move right out already!"

He strolled over, leaned against the doorjamb, and glanced in before meeting her glittering eyes. "It's big, it's furnished, and it has its own bathroom."

"Which doesn't work!"

His eyes lit up with laughter. "You're actually admitting there're plumbing problems in Weatherby House?" he needled. Before she could think of a suitably stinging reply, he straightened and put a firm hand to the small of her back, pushing her into his bedroom.

She gasped and stepped forward, wanting only to escape the warm strength of the hand that burned through the thin material of her dress.

"Take another look around. Not really all that bad, is it?" he said easily.

"Coming from you, that's quite a concession," she snapped and heard a click that brought her sharply around. Blake was extracting an old skeleton key from the closed door.

"What do you think you're doing?" she managed with a startled gasp. Every muscle in her body tensed as he pushed the key into the front pocket of his jeans and smiled at her.

"Another asset of this bedroom is the lock on the door for privacy," he said simply, and she could feel the color seep from her face and then flood back in as he began to slowly unbutton his workshirt and pull it free of his jeans.

"What're you doing?" she squeaked, eyes wide.

"You're repeating yourself. And I'd think it was obvious. I'm taking off my shirt."

And he did, revealing a distressingly broad chest covered with curly black hair that arrowed down over a flat, firm stomach and disappeared beneath the buckle of his leather belt.

"Let me out of here," she demanded, taking a step toward the door.

"Don't panic." He tossed the shirt on an old wing chair. He seemed blatantly amused at her growing discomfort and embarrassment. She couldn't seem to look anywhere else but at him. She clenched her hands in frustration.

"Is this your idea of a frontal assault?" She had meant it to sound insulting, yet somehow it came out sounding shaky and uncertain.

His brows rose faintly and he hooked his thumbs into his belt as he contemplated her worried face for one long, distracting moment.

She stared back, unable to prevent herself from looking down over his body in pulsing awareness. Contrary to every cruel, deliberately hurtful word Rob Hanford had said about her when she gave his ring back, Carla realized with an electric jolt that her libido wasn't dead at all, but alive and well and making itself very uncomfortably felt. Could Blake see how her breath caught, her heart raced? Her muscles tensed in her stomach, and she felt a rush of liquid fire.

Blake's expression changed as he watched her face.

The dark brown eyes lost their mocking humor and grew velvety, glowing with an inner heat that quickened her own breathing even more.

She held out a trembling hand, palm up. "Give me that key, Blake." Her voice was noticeably husky.

Slowly he unhooked his thumbs from his belt and came toward her. "Take it."

"This isn't funny!" she cried out, retracting her hand when he started to reach for it. She backed up, but he caught her shoulders.

"No, it isn't." He searched her face, his own pale and taut. "I was only planning to change my shirt before I took you out, but I don't think I want to take you anywhere tonight after all." He pulled her forward, his mouth swooping down hungrily to take hers. Her head went back with the force of his kiss, even as her hips arched forward. Her hand flattened against his chest, intending to push him away and then spreading instead, feeling the crisp hair and the smooth skin, as his own heart raced even faster than hers.

Groaning, he caught hold of her wrists and pulled her hands out, so that she came full against him. His mouth left hers, trailing hotly across her cheek, then down the curve of her jaw, nudging her until her head went back and she gave him access to the hollow at the base of her throat. He let go of her hands and they went up around his neck. He raised his head, his eyes boring into hers with an intensity that made her breath come out sharply. She pulled him down to kiss her again, hands raking through his hair as she slanted her head, opening her mouth beneath his to deepen the kiss.

His hands tightened convulsively on her back, jerking her closer, holding her body against his. Then one hand moved down over her buttocks, coursing over her hip, along the curve of her waist, and up to cup her breast and seek the hard tip with his thumb. He groaned, kissing her harder. The buttons of her dress were opened one by one, and then Blake was arching her back, his mouth coming down and closing hotly on a nipple, rolling it, nibbling it, drawing it in as she cried out, her head going back, eyes closing. The gentle edge of his teeth against her soft skin drove her wild.

His mouth moved upward over her collarbone, along the pulsing artery in her neck, across her jaw to take her mouth again in a fierce, urgent kiss. She felt his hard knee pressing determinedly between her legs.

She pulled her head back. "No . . ."

"Yes," he groaned, his fingers in her long hair, dragging her mouth back to his. Every nerve and cell in Carla's body was agreeing with him. His strong hands moved to her hips, pulling her against him even harder, then stroking up and down as a primitive muscular pulsing began between them. She could feel his tumescence through her clothes, and the blood seemed to rush in her ears.

Blake's hands shook as he pushed the dress off her shoulders and down to her waist, following its course with his mouth. The rose belt dropped to the floor, followed with alacrity by the soft silk dress. Her hands spread over Blake's broad back, feeling the rippling muscles as he undressed her. When his hands slid beneath the waistband of her half-slip and pantyhose and began pushing them down slowly over her hips, she tensed, her hands retracting and grabbing at his bulging biceps, trying to push him back.

"No, don't," she murmured pleadingly.

He didn't take his hands away, but tightened them so that she was brought forward again, feeling the full length of his heated, aroused body.

"Oh, God, Blake . . . This is *crazy!*" she rasped, her body trembling.

His arms came hard around her, and he was so big that she felt enfolded, her senses reeling from the musky, male scent of his body. Her lips parted, her tongue tasting the warm, tanned skin, faintly salty. He raked his fingers through her hair, pulling her head back.

"Crazy, yes," he said, kissing her again with an urgency that sent a responsive surge of quivering heat spiraling downward into her loins. "Crazy wonderful . . . crazy wild." His voice was deep and breathy.

"We can't," she moaned, trying to drag her mouth away, trying to think.

He pulled her back. "We are."

"Blake, please . . ."

"I've wanted this ever since I saw you in the meeting room." His hands came up, cupping her face, forcing her to meet his raw, passionate look. "I've wanted to kiss you, to touch and taste every inch of you . . . And I'm going to," he warned her, his lips covering hers again, opening her mouth to his. His tongue ran along the inner edge of her teeth and then circled her own.

Then he let her go and drew back, allowing a space between them, and piercing disappointment shook her. She opened her eyes, looking at his back in confusion as he turned and stepped away. Then she saw him close the suitcases with a thud, snap the latches, and swing them off the bed.

Her heart raced as he faced her. She stared at him, recognizing and acknowledging his eyes with every cell and fiber in her body. The dark, burning look in his eyes. He came back for her and she put her arms out, reaching for him instinctively, coming hard against him, hearing and feeling the tempo of his quickened breathing, his thundering heart. When his mouth took hers, she shuddered. Everything in her was coming alive, responding to the sheer maleness of him. He wanted her, and oh God how she wanted him. When had it happened? Or had it always been this way?

Thought was suspended as Blake carried her to the bed and they came down together, arms clinging, legs tangled. Feeling and sensation predominated, wild, triumphant. His hands went to the waistband of her underwear. Her head went back against the mattress, her body arching in a primeval plea. Blake answered with a swift, determined motion, removing the barriers to get to her. He was above, on, in; a deep groan wrenched from him as she clung to his body. He pressed her down, filled, and yet lifted her, too.

"Open your eyes," he murmured raggedly. "Open

your mouth . . . open everything . . . wide, wide." He groaned and kissed her fiercely, deeply, as she gave. Everything in her centered on the warm, wonderful feel of his mouth; the hard, hot pressure of his body; the rhythm; the spiral, the tingling bursting inferno; the sobbing cry; the final aching sigh.

"Carrie . . ." he breathed wondrously.

Magnificent, was all she could think.

"Your face . . ." he whispered against her lips.

And his. Oh, the look at that moment, the way his eyes had centered, gone all black, drawn her in and through.

She felt stunned, in an odd kind of mental shock as her body made the slow downward climb from fulfillment. His body was still hard, warm, and so natural in possession. When he raised his head from her shoulder and looked down at her, he seemed young and heart-stoppingly handsome. His brown eyes were warm and velvety as he smiled down at her, then gently brushed the tousled hair back from her damp temples.

"Do you have room service in this inn of yours?" he asked, lightly kissing the corner of her mouth.

She was staring up at him, coming out of the enchantment, her mind whirling and railing in self-condemnation. What was she doing sprawled beneath him like this? What had she done?

Blake's expression changed slightly as he watched her face. "Carrie, don't . . ."

She gulped, attacked by a quick mortified onslaught of hot tears.

"Carrie," he whispered hoarsely, frowning, holding

her face firmly when she tried to turn away. She closed her eyes tightly.

"Let go," she choked, shaking with aftershock.

"No," he said, and when she tried frantically to extricate herself, he flattened her back with the heavy length of his body. She tried to push and then roll him off, but he caught her wrists, forcing them back against the mattress with painful determination.

She glared up at him in futile self-recrimination. "Slam-bam, thank-you-ma'am?"

His eyes ignited in anger. "Don't say that. It's not the way I see it!"

"No?"

"Hell, no!"

She laughed and pressed her quivering lips together against the unnatural sound of it and shook her head back and forth.

"It might have happened a little fast . . ."

"Might have?" she managed, her throat closing off more.

He searched her agonized face. His eyes softened. "It was connection—pure, complete connection."

"Was it?"

He sighed softly. "Carrie, how did you ever get to be so damn vulnerable? What's going on in your head?"

"Everybody's vulnerable," she told him shakily. "Let me up." She tried to free herself again, but he held her down.

Incensed and frightened by the power of her feelings, she attacked. "Was this little scene part of your master plan to get your way with Weatherby House?"

"To hell with Weatherby House," he snarled. "Lady, don't you ever think of anything else?"

She drew in a sobbing breath, wanting only to get away, to hide. "Let go."

"Carrie, damn it, listen to me," he said through clenched teeth. "I wanted you, yes. I've never made a state secret out of that. Sure, I intended to make love to you, but I damn well didn't intend . . ." He jerked her hard. "Stop squirming and listen to me!" He pulled both hands beneath her, holding them tightly with one of his while with the other he forced her chin up.

"You're twenty-eight—a woman. I'm a man. We wanted each other. We made love. We connected with one another. That doesn't happen every time people make love. It was something beautiful."

"Beautiful?" she sneered and then laughed, frightened, her eyes moist. "It was sordid. It shouldn't have happened at all—not between us," she said tremulously.

His face was pale and rigid. "Why not? Because you can't cope with what it means?"

"It doesn't mean a thing!"

He looked at her for one breath-stopping moment, burning anger replacing all his tender feelings. Then Carla found herself free, the bed jerking and creaking violently as he got up and moved away. She pushed herself up shakily and saw him stepping into his shorts and pants, rebuckling his belt. He cast her a blazing look, and she lowered her eyes. She saw her own clothes—the bikini panties, pantyhose, and half-slip still together and inside out—blatant, humiliating testimony to how quickly everything had transpired.

We couldn't wait for sanity.

Blake came across the room, shrugging on his shirt. She shrank back as he leaned down, looking at her, impaling her with his eyes. His mouth was hard, uncompromising, and she felt renewed tears threaten. His face was dark with anger and something more. Hurt? Disappointment?

He leaned closer, and her heart tripped a jackhammer beat as she huddled there on the bare bed, legs modestly drawn up and turned to one side, arms crossed, hands clenched over her chest. Blake's mouth tightened even more, a muscle jerking in his jaw.

"I'll tell you something, Carla Gelsey," he said grimly. "To me making love to you was beautiful, something special, something real. Now if you'd rather look at yourself as a cheap lay, go ahead. It's your inalienable right to make yourself unhappy, isn't it? If that's the way you'd like to see yourself, there's not much I can do about it, is there?"

He straightened and turned away. He stood there for a half second, almost indecisive, then muttered a short, foul word before striding across the room. He dug into his pocket for the skeleton key and unlocked the door; but before opening it he looked back at her again. Afraid he'd read her confusion of emotions, she covered her face with one shaking hand.

"Just to ease that little high-school mentality of yours, no one will know what's happened between us unless *you* decide to tell." He yanked the door open, and Carla fully expected him to slam it loudly enough for everyone to hear. He didn't. He drew it closed quietly, and she heard his footsteps go down the hall and then the stairs.

Crying softly, she hastily gathered up her discarded clothing and fled through the inner door to the adjoining bedroom.

Chapter Nine

Tossing her silk dress and underthings into the laundry basket, she rummaged through the refinished 1890's dresser she had bought at a garage sale. Crying silently, she pulled on brown slacks, a pullover bulky-knit sweater of dark green and rust, and stepped into casual shoes. Her hands shook as she brushed the wild tangles from her waist-length hair before French-braiding it.

Glancing in the beveled mirror, she knew she had to do something about her face. It was pale, with red splotches from crying. Where was her tote bag with her toiletries? She found it in the hallway outside Blake's door. Grabbing it up, she retreated hastily to the bath-room. Cold water and makeup made the necessary repairs, and she felt ready to escape Weatherby House and Blake Mercer for a few precious hours.

As she came down the stairs, she heard voices in the parlor. Michelle and Sam were talking, their words indistinct but their tone indicating amusement. Mary and Marvin joined in their shared laughter. Carla heard Blake's contagious chuckles as well and felt her chest squeeze painfully. Opening the front door, she went out quietly and quickly, not ready to face anyone yet.

She had to think. She had to sort her feelings out.

Walking along Main Street, she felt close to tears again. What was wrong with her? It wasn't as though this had been her first time with a man. She'd lost her virginity to a college quarterback when she was twenty. They had gone together for over a year and he had finally managed to wear down her principles through a combination of logic and emotional pressure. "If you really love me," he had said, and she really thought she did. It had happened in the back seat of his new car following the big game in which he led the university team to victory against their archrivals. They had both been jubilant but the experience had destroyed all that. He'd lacked control, she'd lacked passion, and the entire affair had been a miserable sham. They'd both told each other it was wonderful, but two weeks later they'd split up.

The only other man she'd ever been with sexually was Rob Hanford. It had taken him a year and a half to get her into bed, and by that time she had been wearing his diamond solitaire and the wedding date had been set for June. The experience with Rob had been no more satisfying than the one with her college boyfriend. Oh, he was vastly more experienced and had remarkable control, yet somehow she had still lacked passion.

When she'd found Rob in bed with another woman

just a few weeks later, she'd simply removed the ring and tossed it on the bed between them before walking out. He'd gotten up and followed her, catching hold of her in his living room, and shouted as though the whole sordid affair had been entirely her fault.

"If you were a woman and not some cold fish, I wouldn't have to go to someone else!" he told her brutally. "I want a woman who wants me, but when I make love to you I wonder if you're thinking about the latest rehab project you're into or if you're calculating your work schedule for the next morning. You're just not there!"

She'd left in tears, feeling shattered more by Rob's dismissal of her own womanhood than by the fact that she had just caught him *flagrante delicto*.

Later, Rob had tried to talk to her. He'd sent flowers every day for two weeks, a dozen red roses a day. Her apartment had begun to look like a funeral parlor. Then he'd sent the ring by messenger, along with a letter assuring her that they could work everything out. She'd returned both with her own short, sweet missal: "Flush them." Rob Hanford hadn't tried to contact her again. Shortly after, she heard that he'd moved in with the woman who'd been in his bed. She also heard, that the woman had been just one of many during their year-long engagement.

Her experiences dating other men in the year that followed led Carla to believe what Rob had said about her. Maybe she *was* lacking as a woman. Maybe she couldn't be aroused by anyone. She wasn't even sure she wanted to be. But then one touch and a burning look from dark brown eyes had put an end to all those suppositions. One kiss and she'd tumbled backwards like a tipped-over turtle.

Blake Mercer represented everything she'd been fighting against for the past seven years. Give the man carte blanche and he'd probably tear down the world and rebuild it with synthetic materials and prefabs! But, oh lordy, how wildly he'd made her body sing to his tune; and when he'd looked down at her after she came down from the heavens, he had made her feel for one amazed moment that he could do anything he wanted— with her and with the world—if only he'd make her feel like that again!

Carla blinked to contain threatening tears. This was crazy! Had he managed to parboil her brains when he made love to her in that musty upstairs bedroom or what?

The street and neon lights were on up and down Main. Bronco Sam's beckoned in glaring red with a gold lasso. Common sense told her to give it a wide berth, but some self-destructive tendency made her push open the swinging door and enter the dim interior.

A mechanical bull stood in the center of the place, surrounded by thick mats. A long oak bar with brass footrail ran along the back. The bartender looked up from drying glasses. He was in his fifties, dressed like a cowhand, and sported an incredible handlebar mustache. There were a dozen others in the place, all blending in, having their drinks on the way home from work. Several glanced curiously across at her, following her progress as she wove her way between small oak tables and took a seat at one of the booths along the back wall. The room was dark paneled with tack hanging about and wagonwheel lights turned down low. Apparently a band played there on occasion, for there were drums, a mike, and several chairs set up in one corner and a large planked square for dancing. At the moment, however, a jukebox was playing a popular country-western tune.

Carla had never been partial to country-western and wondered why she had entered in the first place. Self-punishment, she decided, when one of the men at the bar sauntered over, dropped in a quarter, and punched out several other twangy tunes.

The bartender stood by her booth, and she decided not to insult him by leaving. One drink and she'd go.

"What can I get you, honey?" he asked in a broad Texas drawl. Then his eyes narrowed in hostile recognition. "Hey, aren't you the broad that bought the old Weatherby place?"

She groaned inwardly and looked up with a forced smile. "Guilty as charged."

"Lady, I advise you to get yourself on out of here," he told her grimly.

"Are you telling me you won't serve me?"

He leaned down and put his hands on the table. "You kept some good men out of work by buying that dump out from under Blake Mercer. They won't take kindly to you coming in their place."

She sighed. "I didn't intend to put anyone out of work. I only want to preserve something very special, something Allandale won't see ever again."

"You're not leaving?" he demanded, apparently not the least interested in her opinion.

She looked up at him impatiently. "No, I am not leaving."

He shrugged indifferently and straightened. "Okay, lady. Just don't claim I didn't warn you. Now name your poison."

Since she seldom drank at all, she wasn't sure what she wanted to order. She doubted they would have much of a selection of white wine, though they probably stocked every brand of whiskey and beer known to man.

The man raised thick, grizzled brows impatiently. "I got other customers waiting, in case you didn't notice. Now how's about making up your mind before Tuesday next week."

She smiled. "A sloe gin fizz."

His expression showed what he thought of her choice. "Brady does those drinks and he's out on his dinner break."

"What's your specialty?" She could guess.

"Plain fare. The only mixing I do is with water, tonic, or club soda."

"How about a beer?" she asked sweetly.

"Yup. What kind you want?"

"How many kinds do you have?"

"I haven't got all night, lady."

"Whatever you have handy is fine," she muttered, giving up. She sighed in relief when he went away. He mumbled something to the men at the bar and took down a sizable glass mug. There was low laughter. Two of the men glanced across at her, and she wondered if she'd somehow been set up. Gritting her teeth, she decided she'd pay for the beer, drink it, and leave.

The bartender brought back a tall, frothy beer.

"What's this?" she asked when he set the brew down ceremoniously in front of her. She was well aware of the others watching and grinning.

"House specialty: Bronco's Boilermaker. All the construction workers around here love 'em. They put hair on your chest."

"Frankly, I don't want any hair on my chest."

He grinned at that. "Well, in that case maybe it'll make a woman out of you."

She could refuse to take up his challenge and lose face, as the spectators hoped, or she could be a good sport and drink it. Meeting the bartender's eyes, she tipped her head back and took two long pulls of beer. Her eyes watered. "Did I pass muster with your cronies at the bar?" she asked, her voice hoarse.

"You've still got some beer left, but I'll ask them. Did you want something else?" he asked politely, grinning broadly now as she drained her glass.

She was having trouble getting air down her windpipe. She shook her head and pointed to the empty glass. "How much do I owe you?"

"Didn't think you could handle it. It's on the house."

132

"Thanks."

She watched him balefully as he walked back to the bar. He said something to the men, and they laughed again. A muscular man in his mid-thirties turned on his stool to look at her. He was dressed in old jeans, a faded blue denim shirt, and construction boots. He drank his beer while watching her, and Carla pretended not to notice. After a word to the bartender, he took up his glass and headed toward her. Carla tensed.

The man slid onto the bench facing her and looked at her with unconcealed dislike. "You did me out of badly needed work, Miss Gelsey," he said directly. "I've got a wife and three kids to support. You want to tell me what I do now?"

She almost blurted out that he could put the money spent on beer to better use, but decided that might earn her a punch in the nose. She looked up at him and saw the troubled hazel eyes, the bitter depression. Sighing, she frowned. "I'm sorry," she said frankly.

He seemed surprised by her simple apology, but apparently he still had a few things to say. "I'm not the only one. Who do you think you are, coming into town and blasting all our plans to hell? That project the city council had planned for us would've put bread on several tables and paid some mortgages." He pushed his half-finished beer to one side so he could lean forward. "Now I have to take unemployment."

"Keep your voice down, Frank," another man said, and Carla looked up in alarm to see three others approaching—all big, all unfriendly, all with battle

133

shining in their narrowed eyes. One was in his mid-forties, lean and hard with gray at the temples and a wide mouth. The creases indicated he smiled frequently, but he wasn't smiling now. Another was younger, probably about thirty, tall and broad, with hair thinning at the top. The third looked to be in his twenties and wore brown cords and a plaid western shirt. The buckle of his belt had COORS on it. He put his booted foot on the end of Carla's bench, cutting off any escape she might have made.

The bartender brought over a tray of drinks. "Thanks, Sam," Frank said and nodded toward Carla. Sam put down another boilermaker.

She glanced up. "I didn't order this."

"I did," Frank told her.

"If you don't drink it, he might take it as a personal insult," the youngest man said with a faint smile.

The older man straddling a chair grinned at her maliciously. "Drink up, honey. It's the neighborly thing to do."

Carla Gelsey, you idiot! Why did you ever set foot in this place?

"You caused a lot of ill-luck, you know that, lady," Frank said. "You do us out of honest work and then import your own scabs."

"What do you do with that long-haired creep you moved in with you, huh?" the older man said insinuatingly.

The younger man leaned forward. "And who's the broad with the illegitimate kid?"

134

"Not to mention the other hippie-type she's got living there with her."

"Right on Main Street, rubbing our noses in it," the last put in.

"Lady," Frank began again, "we ought to burn you and your bunch out."

Looking around at the circle of men hemming her in, Carla knew that Blake hadn't exaggerated the animosity felt by some Allandale citizens. She had been amused at the time, hardly taking him seriously, but these men were deadly serious.

"Well, haven't you got anything to say?" the older man put in. "You had plenty to say at the city council meeting a few weeks ago. Couldn't shut you up then. What've you got to say now?"

She swallowed slowly, hoping they wouldn't see how they intimidated her. "What would you have me say?"

Frank laughed shortly and downed his beer. The young man glanced at him, then rested his forearms on his raised knee. "That you're selling out, packing up and leaving," he told her truthfully.

They were all looking at her, waiting. She looked back and saw four men, out of work, miserable and worried. The one had said he was married with children. She felt sad. Worse, she felt guilty.

"Well?" Frank demanded, glaring at her.

She moistened her dry lips and tugged on the top one nervously with her bottom teeth. Putting her palms on the table, she let her breath out slowly. "I'm not selling. I'm not packing, and I'm not leaving."

"Maybe we ought to do something to change your mind, hmmm?" Frank threatened. He looked at the young man with his boot on her bench. "Terry, got any suggestions?" Terry smiled faintly. Frank passed on to the older man sitting. "Floyd, how about you?" Then to the man sitting next to him on the opposite bench, he said, "Jack, here's your chance."

Carla frowned, heart thundering. "Like what? Fire-bomb the house or maybe lynch me at sunrise?" she called their bluff. Or was it a bluff?

"It's a thought, lady," Frank said flatly, looking at her squarely. Her eyes widened slowly, her face paling.

"I think you're scaring her, Frank," Terry said, still holding that faint smile.

She looked around at all of them. "Wasn't that what you gentlemen had in mind? A little hometown vigi-lante intimidation? Four men against one woman. That makes your odds about right, doesn't it?" Her heart was pumping fast and hard, and she knew they could see how badly frightened she was. Let them see. "Just for the record, you've succeeded. Satisfied?"

Frank's steely gaze wavered slightly, and she sensed he was ashamed. He nudged the man beside him. "Come on, let's go back to the bar."

They all avoided looking at her as they stood up slowly. Suddenly Carla understood something she hadn't considered before. They were scared too. People did things they wouldn't normally do when they were under severe stress.

Acting on impulse, she reached across the small table

and put her hand on Frank's arm. "Don't leave yet. Please."

He jerked at her touch and then stared at her in surprise. She took her hand away and looked at the others. "All of you," she expanded. "Please. Just sit down and let me talk to you for a few minutes. Let me try to explain why Weatherby House means so much to me—and what it could mean to Allandale." They hesitated, and she tried again. "I'll sweeten the offer with a couple of rounds of drinks," she suggested, giving them a faint, coaxing smile.

A long talk didn't swing them over to her side, but at least they were less hostile. Four rounds of drinks had helped. Carla was feeling no pain herself, having managed the second boilermaker and then nursed another beer.

Carla was defending Marvin. "He's a licensed carpenter, one of the best in the restoration business."

"How much you paying him?" Floyd asked. "Union wages?"

"Room and board," Carla answered honestly. "He was out of work, too."

"Miss Gelsey, you're a cheap boss," Terry said, but a thin smile took the edge off his insult.

"I'd pay him more if I had it," she said with a shrug. "But almost everything I have is going for materials to restore the house. I'm helping them by giving them free room and board until they find jobs, and they're helping me by giving their expertise to the house."

"He'd get a job if he cut his hair and shaved off that bush on his face," Frank grumbled.

She looked across the table at him. "You have short hair and no beard. How come you aren't working?"

"I'd be working if you hadn't bought that place out from under Mercer's committee."

"Weren't you out of work already?" she asked, two shots of whiskey and three beers giving her the courage to do so.

"Yeah. But—"

"Drink your beer and change the subject," Floyd broke in, following his own advice.

The bar was filling up. The noise was as thick as the smoke. A small band was playing, but no one was dancing. Several men had ridden the mechanical bull. Carla had enough money left for a telephone call. If she had another boilermaker, she'd probably need it to phone someone and have them come drag her out from under the table. She looked at the four men still sitting with her. They had told her their problems, and she'd shared some of her own. Nothing had been settled, but at least they were more friendly now.

"What do I have to do to be sure y'all won't firebomb my house?" she asked bluntly, suppressing a hiccup.

Frank considered her over his beer and gave her a malicious smile. "Ride Samson for thirty seconds."

"Samson?"

"The bull," Terry enlightened her.

"What bull?" she asked, playing dumb.

"That bull," Floyd answered, jerking his thumb

138

toward the center of the room. She glanced over just in time to see a man being pitched through the air to bounce on the mat with a loud grunt.

"That's what I was afraid of," Carla murmured, and the four men laughed. "All right," she said, taking them up on it. "If that's the payment for my insurance policy, I'll do it."

Terry slid off the bench to let her up.

"After I finish this beer," she told him. They laughed again as she took a long, theatrical gulp before following Terry.

After Floyd's loud announcement at the mike, everyone in Bronco Sam's knew who she was and why she was riding the bull. She lasted six seconds and the room was loud with unrestrained cheers and applause at her failure. Weatherby House had no champions, apparently. None but herself.

"Too bad about that," Frank said, grinning broadly as he gave her a hand and pulled her up.

"Not so fast, buster," she said, winded. "Didn't say anything about how many tries I got." She rubbed her hands together and climbed back up.

Frank shook his head, disbelieving. "Suit yourself." He dropped more change in the machine and it started off again.

This time Carla lasted ten seconds. There was more laughter and applause. "Atta boy, Samson! Give her hell!"

"You're not going to try it again, are you?" Floyd said in obvious amazement. "You sure you didn't land

139

on your head the first time?"

She rubbed her posterior and gave him a rueful smile. "Definitely not my head."

It took four more tries before Carla lasted the full thirty seconds. At the thirty-first second she and the machine parted ways again, it rocking gleefully on while she flew head-first through the air, flipped, and landed flat on her back. There were audible gasps from the onlookers.

Carla remained there for a moment, getting her wind back. "You okay?" Frank asked, hunkering down beside her, looking concerned. She pushed herself up on her elbows and gave him a lopsided grin.

"You drive a hard bargain, Frank."

He grinned back. "You made the thirty seconds."

"And you gave your word you'd leave me and my house in peace," she reminded him.

He held out his hand. "You got it." She took his hand and grimaced as he helped her up. The four men wove their way back through the tables to the booth with her. Carla heard some people clap for her, but most of them still probably wished she'd broken her neck. After talking to the four men, she supposed she could understand why. But it changed nothing. Maybe when Weatherby House was restored to its full glory they would understand.

She took up her purse. "You know, gentlemen, I won't lie and say this evening has been a *total* pleasure." She smiled teasingly, and they laughed with her. Floyd patted her on the back, and she winced and rolled her eyes at them.

"Your Samson ought to be gelded," she muttered, and they laughed again.

"You need someone to see you home?" Terry asked, putting his work-toughened hand beneath her wrist. She shook her head.

"No, thanks. I'm fine."

"Lady," Frank said, "I don't agree with one damn thing you said about that place, but I admire your determination."

The words brought a lump to her throat. She nodded as she put a hand on his arm. She swallowed. "However tactless I sounded at that meeting, I never intended to hurt anyone with this project. I hope you'll change your mind when I open the place to the public."

"Something will come along." He shrugged, but she could see in all their eyes that times were bad, and the future for them and their families was grim.

When she went outside, the cool late-night air assaulted her system. She was well oiled, she decided, sucking in air and hoping it would sober her up. It didn't. In fact, all that air seemed to go straight to her head.

She decided to stop at an all-night donut shop at the far end of town. The young Chinese woman who waited on her was polite but curious as she watched Carla sway into the shop, look over the selection, and give her order.

"Ooops, I forgot. One slim dime is all I've left," Carla said with a grin. "Will you take this instead of the green stuff?" She held up her checkbook. The girl nodded, giving her a disapproving look. Carla wrote out a check, tore it off with a flourish, and presented it with a deep bow. "Thank you. Thank you," she said as she picked up the box of bearclaws and headed out the door.

Making her way back down Main Street, Carla started chuckling to herself. Whoever said one couldn't walk off two boilermakers and a few extra beers? Come now, girl, she urged herself, walk that straight line down the sidewalk.

The gate before Weatherby House seemed stuck. After two fumbling tries to open it, she tucked the donut box under her arm and swung her leg up and over. As she straddled the gate precariously, she heard someone coming down the walkway from the house. Not wanting to be caught in that undignified perch, she lifted the other leg and went toppling over to sprawl on the cobblestone walkway inside the fence. She gave a loud grunt and started to giggle.

"Good lord," Blake muttered. "What happened to you?"

She sat looking at him, lifting one finger to her lips. "Shhhhh! Someone might hear . . ." A peal of laughter emerged like an explosion. Blake stood staring down at her, arms akimbo, mouth curving slightly.

"You're blasted."

"Who? Me?" She made it to her hands and knees.

"What're you doing?"

"Lost something," she muttered, feeling around until her hand contacted the box, luckily still tightly closed.

"Where've you been?" he asked, reaching down to take her arm.

"Promised Marv bearclaws," she slurred, clutching the box as she tried to regain her feet with Blake's help. As she straightened, a loud hiccup issued, and she clapped her hand over her mouth. Blake laughed softly, and she wagged her finger at him. "Shhhhhhhh!" Then she started to laugh again.

Straightening up was a mistake. Everything went rolling and tipping. She felt Blake's strong arm around her waist. "Hey!"

"Goo . . . night . . ." she murmured and passed out.

Chapter Ten

She woke up in her room. The adjoining door to Blake's room was open. Groaning, she pushed herself up from her air mattress and sleeping bag. Pain shot through what she calculated to be every muscle in her body. Breath hissed through clenched teeth, and she sank back with eyes closed.

"Good morning," Blake said from the doorway. "How're you feeling?"

She opened one eye carefully and mouthed the words, "Go away."

"You'll feel better if you get up and move around a little." He came across the room. "I brought you some coffee."

She was sitting up before she realized she wasn't

wearing anything by flimsy bikini panties. She pulled the sleeping bag up and winced sharply. Blake had been smiling, but his eyes narrowed as he spotted a mark on her shoulder. "By the way, what happened to your back?" He set the mug down and came around her. He pulled at the sleeping bag.

"What're you doing?"

He yanked it down and unzipped it as well. She gasped, and just that much sound and movement shot through her head like a thunderbolt.

Blake swore softly. "You're bruised all over," he rasped. "What in hell happened to you last night?" His hand was warm on her thigh as she kept her arms crossed over her full breasts.

"Samson happened," she murmured, gritting her teeth.

"Samson who?"

"Samson the bull, that's who."

"Bull! Have you been out running around in someone's field?"

"Do you have to shout? Couldn't you be nice and write notes?" She grimaced, hands clutching her head.

"What bull? Where and how?" he ground out quietly.

"The one at Bronco Sam's," she answered bleakly, eyeing him for a reaction.

He stared at her with dawning comprehension. "*That* bull! That's the last place I'd have expected you to go."

"I won't be going back, I guarantee." She smiled ruefully.

His gaze moved from her reddened eyes down over her bruised body and back up to linger on her breasts.

She pulled the flap of the sleeping bag back up. "Do you mind?" she managed indignantly, even those words making her head throb abominably.

He straightened, and she looked up the powerful, heady length of him. "I'll give you a few minutes to get dressed."

"Who said I'm getting up?"

"A workaholic like you?" He grinned and closed the door behind him.

Carla sat in a warm bath for almost an hour before she felt able to get dressed and go to work. She couldn't face the thought of physical labor, so she made her way up to the attic to begin sorting through boxes of old papers. Mary had given her the okay to peruse whatever was up here. She could hear the others using power sanders somewhere below. Until the materials for the shingles arrived, they had agreed to work on the kitchen.

Finding several boxes of old file folders and miscellaneous letters, Carla toted them downstairs into her small bedroom, which had better light and was more comfortable. It made six trips, and with each one the stack of boxes against the wall grew.

She needed a break, more coffee, and something to put into her queasy stomach, so she decided to go downstairs for a break. As she was walking along the dim hallway she saw that Mary's door was open so she stuck her head inside.

"Hi, Mary. Everything all right with you this morning?" she said with forced cheerfulness. The power saw began again in the kitchen. "Ohhhh . . ." she groaned, gritting her teeth and squeezing her eyes shut. She felt as if the machine was being used on her own head.

"Carrie!" Mary cried, pleased to see her. "Come in, dear. Come in!"

Carla did, closing the door quickly to muffle the high-pitched whir. She put a hand on her forehead as she leaned back to steady herself against the closed door.

"You look like death warmed over, dear," Mary said.

"Sit down," Blake ordered, and too late Carla opened her eyes and saw him sitting in the other chair, legs stretched out in front of him as he looked at her in wry amusement. "How's the head?"

"There." It wasn't just her head that hurt, however, and the thought of sitting on the remaining oak chair was less than enticing.

Blake apparently understood. "Try Mary's bed. It's soft."

"Thanks," she grunted. "I'll stand."

"Have you seen this yet?" Mary chortled, rattling the newspaper she'd been reading. "You made the Allandale *Tribune*."

"*What?*"

"There's even a picture of you. Look!"

Blake watched as she moved carefully across the room and leaned down to see what Mary was laughing about. Her face paled even more when she saw the picture and headline—on the front page no less: SAMSON TOSSES GELSEY it read, and below was a big picture of

146

her doing the last midair somersault, arms and legs flying in all directions. She closed her eyes in dismay.

"They must have been short on news," she murmured. "Why else would they have put something so ridiculous on their front page?"

"You're underrating yourself," Blake drawled. "Since you hit Allandale, you've been big news, all right." She tried to ignore him, but couldn't help glancing his way. Her dismay increased with each word she read. His brown eyes glinted with laughter and she saw he was noting the motto on her pale green T-shirt: FESTINA LENTE: "Make haste slowly."

He stood. "I'll take you out for something to eat."

Her defenses went up as unwanted memories of yesterday afternoon in the upstairs bedroom flooded her senses and colored her cheeks. "Maybe I already ate!"

His smile was a mocking challenge. "You've been in the attic and your bedroom going through boxes of records."

Was he keeping tabs on her? "I can make something for myself, thank you. There's no need—"

"I don't think you could survive the noise," he told her, and his expression made it clear that he was not about to take no for an answer.

Mary patted Carla's hand distractedly as she looked at the paper. "Go on, dear. Don't fight it."

Blake grinned. Carla blushed hotly.

"Did you really drink half a dozen boilermakers?" Mary asked, and Carla bent down closer.

"Does it say I did?" she gasped, appalled.

147

"Right there, in black printer's ink. 'One bystander said he saw more than half a dozen boilermakers delivered to Carla Gelsey's booth.'"

"For crying out loud, there were four men there with me!" Carla protested the unfair reporting, incensed.

Mary glanced up sharply. "*Four?* My goodness. Now you sit down right there and tell me everything!" Her eyes brightened with avid interest.

"Later, Aunt Mary," Blake said, standing. "She's got one foot in the grave and the other on a banana peel." He took Carla's arm firmly.

The din in the hallway as they left Mary's room convinced Carla that Blake was right. She wouldn't survive the noise. She went with him without further argument, acutely aware of his hand at the small of her back. Once in his car, he put the key in the ignition and then turned to look at her with piercing, merciless eyes.

"What's the matter? Are you out of gas?" she quipped nervously, and then felt her heart knocking out of tune when he didn't smile at all. He looked angry.

"Did you get smashed last night because we made love?"

The attack couldn't have been more direct, and she felt unable to face it. She turned away, hoping he would drop the subject. But in his usual arrogant manner, he wanted to see every agonized expression on her face. His hand beneath her chin brought her head back around again. "Well, Carrie?"

His voice and touch were so gentle that she felt close to tears. "Partly," she admitted huskily.

He stroked her jaw with the back of his knuckles and started the Jaguar with a roar. "We'll feed you first, then go someplace quiet and talk."

He drove her to Kendicot's Café at the far end of town. As soon as they walked in, Carla could tell that several people had heard all about the night before. A highway patrolman was sitting at the counter reading the paper and laughing with the waitress, who nudged him when she saw Carla. He glanced up.

Blake put both hands lightly on Carla's hips, ushering her—or rather pushing her—in. They took a booth by the front windows. She toyed with the salt and pepper shakers and ran nervous fingers over the paper packets of low-calorie sweetener.

"I think I just lost my appetite."

He reached out and captured her roving hand, his fingers closing around hers. "Relax."

She was aware that the patrolman and waitress were very interested in this new development. She wondered distractedly if they knew that Blake's touch was making her body go all hot and quivery. She remembered those hands on her, caressing her throbbing breasts, stroking and arousing, working wonders on her.

Blake certainly seemed to know. His expression darkened. She retracted her hand sharply, and he smiled slightly. The waitress headed in their direction like a bee to a clover patch, her hazel eyes filled with unveiled interest. She was blond, trim, and very attractive, and Carla wasn't surprised that she and Blake were acquainted.

"Good morning, Sarah."

"Blake. How're you doing? It's been a while."

"I've been working."

Carla took the proffered menu with a bleak smile.

"Coffee for both of us," Blake ordered. "And then a full ranch breakfast for Miss Gelsey here. She needs it."

Sarah laughed softly. "After half a dozen boilermakers at Sam's, you bet." She glanced up from her pad at Blake again. "Nothing else for you?" she asked, pencil poised.

He looked squarely at Carla, eyes glinting. "Not for the moment," he drawled, mouth curving in a suggestive smile. Sarah looked at them with undisguised interest.

"It'll be ready in about ten minutes," she said and returned to the counter. She called the order through to the cook, then went back to chatting with the patrolman.

Carla glared at Blake. "What're you trying to do, create another story?" She lifted her hand as though outlining a headline: " 'Gelsey Plays Footsies with Mercer in Local Café.' "

"Too long. They'd pare it down to 'Mercer Wants Gelsey.' " He looked straight at her as he said it and her heart threatened to burst the bounds of her chest.

"Don't," she whispered frantically.

He looked at her for a long, heart-throbbing moment before relenting. "Tell me what happened to you last night."

She sighed, thankful for the reprieve, and rubbed her

temples with shaky fingers. "I went into that place on impulse and then just couldn't leave."

Blake leaned back, surveying her intently. "Why not?"

"Well"—she hesitated—"the bartender suggested I leave."

He grinned, comprehending. "And in customary Gelsey fashion, you dug your heels in and decided to fight it out."

She narrowed her blue eyes angrily. "I only wanted one beer, but then four of your local gentlemen decided to join me and buy another."

"Your first boilermaker?"

She smiled slightly. "Second. The first one was on the house." She laughed softly, then sobered. "They started out by threatening me, but we all got to talking and we had a few rounds of drinks and—"

"Did you come to any agreement?"

"No, but they said they wouldn't burn me out, or cause trouble, if I could ride Samson for thirty seconds. So I did."

"It said in the paper it took you six tries. You could have broken your neck," he told her grimly.

She shrugged, but even that much movement hurt. Blake shook his head slowly, his mouth curving sardonically. "You'd do damn near anything to save Weatherby House, wouldn't you?"

She looked at him squarely. "It's worth saving, Blake."

"So you keep saying." He sounded no more convinced.

Sarah delivered coffee and a huge breakfast of over-easy eggs, hash-browns, sausage, and toast.

"I can't eat all this," she murmured when Sarah departed.

"Try. You've lost some weight since you came to Allandale."

She had—about seven pounds—but she was surprised he'd noticed. Worry had a way of burning calories.

Blake drank his coffee while Carla worked on her breakfast. It was good, and she found she was very hungry. She finished everything and sat back with a satisfied sigh.

"More coffee?" Sarah asked, pot hovering. Blake shook his head.

"No, thank you," Carla said, smiling. "Everything was delicious, but I can't squeeze in another bite or sip."

"You do look much better," Sarah said frankly, amused. The patrolman had left, and she seemed ready to linger.

"How much do we owe you, Sarah?" Blake asked. Sarah set the coffeepot down on the booth table and took out her pad, tallying the bill and then tearing it off for him. He lifted his lean hips enough to get to his wallet and pay her. "Keep the change."

"Thanks," Sarah said with a bright smile.

Back in Blake's Jaguar, Carla grew nervous again. "Where are we going now?"

"To my place."

"Oh no you don't," she said firmly.

He laughed softly, started the car, backed it out of the parking space, and turned out of town toward the country club.

"Blake, I said *no!*"

"We're only going to talk . . . unless you decide you want to do more."

Fuming, she stared out the window, knowing he would go wherever he wanted no matter what she said.

The narrow two-lane road wove up into the hills. Elegant houses bordered either side, nestled among oaks and pine. There was a golf course, but few people were on the fairways, for it was the middle of the week and mid-morning. The clubhouse was a large chalet-style building. Blake turned onto another road and went up higher, finally bringing the car to a stop at the end of a circular driveway before a large natural-wood house. All the others they had passed had been impressive Tudor, Spanish hacienda, or Mediterranean villa styles, proclaiming to any passerby that the owners had plenty of money to burn. This house was large but simple in design, solid and unassuming yet blending perfectly with the surrounding landscape.

"No steel," Blake told her, withdrawing the key from the ignition, "but plenty of glass."

He ushered her into a large living room and stepped behind a built-in bar. "Would you like a taste of the hair of the dog that bit you?" He grinned.

She was more interested in looking around. The room wasn't as big as she'd first thought, but it gave a feeling of great space. There was a stone fireplace in the middle of the back wall, and on either side were sliding glass doors which opened out onto a wooden deck. Going closer to look out, she saw a hot tub at one end which was positioned so that anyone using it had plenty of privacy but could see out over the country club and Allandale. Turning, she noted that one wall of the room was solid with bookshelves. The other had built-in cabinets with expensive stereo equipment, a television, and V.H.S. A glance around confirmed that Blake liked simple modern furniture built for comfort and that he preferred earth colors.

He was watching her closely, and she gazed at him squarely. "Can I look around at the rest of the house?" she asked, interested.

"Make yourself at home."

The kitchen was small and functional. Everything was within easy reach, and for such a small space there were a surprising number of cabinets. He had all built-in appliances, including a microwave and trash compacter.

There were three bedrooms, each with its own full bath. The master bedroom was at the end of the house and opened onto a deck to the spa. Again Carla was struck by the elegant simplicity of the house. There was no wasted space here, nothing extra, yet there wasn't any feeling of cost cutting either. Everything was made of first-class materials. She opened the sliding glass door from the master suite and stepped out onto the redwood deck. Looking up and around, she noted other features carefully constructed to be inconspicuous.

"Solar?" she asked, glancing back at him.

"Passive and active. I have my own generator as well." No boasting, just a simple statement. It probably wouldn't cost him one month of her utility bills for Weatherby House to heat and cool this place for an entire year, she grudgingly admitted to herself. Everything she had seen was impressive.

"What's the verdict?" He stood, arms crossed over his chest, watching her with a faint smile.

"A little bit of gingerbread might help."

He laughed softly, straightened, dropped his hands to his sides, and came toward her with catlike strides. "Come on, what do you think?"

"It's not a thrown-up tract house built with plasterboard and spit."

"I'll take that as a compliment."

"You designed it, of course."

"And built it."

"All of it?"

"All of it."

Then he was a craftsmen as well as a general contractor, and that couldn't always be said. She began to look at him in a new light—at least professionally. But as he came closer and put his hands on her waist, she stiffened, pulse soaring.

"The spa would help all those battered muscles," he told her softly.

She shook her head and pushed her hands firmly against his forearms, feeling the muscles hard beneath the smooth cotton shirt. Her heart jumped as he smiled, a slow, provocative curve of that sensual mouth.

He let go of her slowly, heading back toward the master bedroom while still looking at her. "I *don't* have a woman's bathing suit, but you can wear one of my T-shirts."

She had half expected, half hoped he would kiss her, but he went back into the house, and she was left to follow. He had opened an armoire drawer. Turning, he tossed a white T-shirt onto the big double bed, which was covered with a brown-and-gold spread. "I'll be back in five minutes."

She chewed on her lower lip for a moment, then shrugged to herself. Why not? It would help. She could be adult about the whole thing, couldn't she?

The water was warm as she stepped in and sat down on the lower ledge so that the jets churned water around her back and hips. She sank lower until only her head was above water, her long braid floating around her as she closed her eyes.

"Don't go to sleep," Blake warned softly, and she opened her eyes in surprise, not having heard him enter. He was sitting opposite her, chest bare, arms stretched out along the rim of the hot tub, watching her with dark, smoldering eyes. Her breasts tingled, and her stomach muscles slowly tightened. She ran a nervous tongue along her lips and swallowed.

"Feel any better?" he asked.

She nodded, afraid to trust the timbre of her voice. "I can't stay long."

His straight, white teeth flashed in a grin. "Carrie,

sometimes you sound like a teenager on her first date."

Her mouth tightened and she sat up, realizing belatedly that her full breasts were visible beneath the wet, clinging T-shirt. She sank down a few inches. "I was simply stating a fact."

"Oh, I know exactly what you were saying," he said easily, still vastly amused by her unease.

"This was a mistake," she grumbled resentfully, wondering how she could manage to get out of the spa without Blake seeing absolutely everything.

"Why?" he demanded roughly, all humor gone in the growing heat of his dark, seductive eyes. Just the way he looked at her made her body throb with warm desire. She lifted her eyes to his.

"Blake, I don't need this kind of complication in my life," she told him truthfully. "I don't think I could deal with it."

"What's complicated?" His face was tight, unyielding.

"You know what I mean," she said desperately.

"The fact that when I touch you, you go all soft inside?"

She blushed hotly.

"I got the feeling yesterday it had never happened like that before," he went on, impaling her with that unwavering look, demanding total honesty.

Her color deepened even more. "You're not being fair," she murmured shakily.

"To hell with being fair," he said, lowering his arms into the water and sliding until his hand closed around her ankle.

"Blake, don't," she gasped, the feel of that hand sending fiery sensations up her leg.

"What complications?" he demanded roughly, his thumb caressing the soft skin at the hollow of her ankle.

"You know what I mean," she whispered, her breathing quickening.

"Frankly, I don't. Enlighten me, Carrie." Her name was a husky caress.

"You. Me. Weatherby House."

His brows rose mockingly. "Is that a love triangle or something?"

She tried to kick his hand away, but he caught her other ankle, pulling her legs across his so that one was on either side of him.

"Let go," she said through gritted teeth. He pulled slowly, and she felt her hips slide down the ledge. Her hands slapped into the water as she desperately sought to grip the edge. "Don't!" Her shoulders went under. He leaned forward, his hands sliding up along her slender legs, catching hold of her slim hips, pulling her across so she was straddling him. She realized with a shock that he was naked.

"Blake!" she cried in frantic protest, but he caught hold of her wet braid and forced her forward again, taking her mouth with ruthless determination. She could feel his hard-muscled legs and the crisp hair beneath her soft thighs. That wasn't all she felt. She struggled fiercely, then realized she was only making matters worse. It was arousing him even faster.

Blake's mouth moved inexorably on hers. He ran the warm, wet tip of his tongue along the edge of her teeth, and, to her utter dismay, it was just like he said. She went all soft inside. Yielding to his will-shattering touch, she opened her mouth to him and slid her arms tightly around his neck, pressing her body even closer. The hand in her hair relaxed, caressing the nape of her neck and then stroking downward. The other moved up from her hip, past her rib cage, and closed over one of her breasts, lightly pinching the hard peak. He dragged his mouth away.

"Just for the record," he rasped against her neck, "yesterday was a new experience for me, too."

"Oh? You were a virgin?"

He laughed against the curve of her neck. "Not quite."

She could feel his heart racing, his breath growing harsh as he stroked her.

"You're not going to try and tell me you go all soft, are you?" she murmured with a husky laugh.

"Carrie, Carrie," he groaned. "Take these damn clothes off, and let me get to you."

She drifted back just enough for him to remove the thin garments, and then he was pulling her back, sinking down, raising his hips up beneath her. Her head went back and she gave a soft, rasping cry.

His hands were firm and strong on her hips. He moved them in a slow, undulating circle while watching her through half-closed dark eyes. "You try to tell me now that this is a complication," he said raggedly. She moaned as he moved her again, raising himself further. Her head fell forward, her breasts coming full against his furred, pounding chest.

"It's happening again. Faster than yesterday," he said against her neck. "Isn't it?"

Their bodies moved together in perfect cooperation. Everything was centering, tight, hot, shaking out of control. She gasped, clutching him, and then felt as though she were suddenly floating free with mind-deadening sensation.

"Open your eyes," he whispered. "Look at me."

His face was taut with desire, his skin faintly flushed. He gritted his teeth, his own dark eyes closing slowly as his head went back and she saw the hard, quick pulse in his throat.

She lifted her hands and caressed his face as he relaxed back with a sigh. He dampened his lips, his breathing still hard, issuing out with sharp sighs. He shook his head slowly, smiling, and then raised it just enough to look at her.

"When we've been together for a while, we'll learn to hold onto that and stretch it out." His hand shook slightly as he cupped one side of her face, his eyes incredibly soft. "God, what you do to me . . ."

She drew back and he let her go, watching her with a faint frown. She caught her panties from the swirling hot water and pulled them on. Then she stepped up out of the hot tub, one arm across her breasts as she felt him still watching her. She went into the master bath for a towel. Blake followed, shrugging into a maroon terrycloth robe he'd draped over a deck chair.

He leaned against the doorjamb. "You can't leave until I'm good and ready to let you," he warned her.

She passed him without meeting his gaze. She picked up her French bra and slipped into it, snapping it at the front. Then she stepped into her faded jeans and pulled her T-shirt on, lifting her long braid free.

"Let's be frank, shall we?" she said, still unable to look at him, feeling a painful lump growing in her throat.

"By all means," he drawled, eyes glowing dangerously.

She swallowed and dampened dry lips before raising her head and facing him squarely. "This attraction between us doesn't change anything, Blake. It just makes things more difficult. You are what you are, and I am what I am."

"Meaning that, since you're into restoration and I'm into designing and building, we can't make it work."

She swallowed again, widening her eyes so the tears wouldn't spill over. "That's about it."

His face softened. "Carrie . . ."

She shook her head. "Don't, please. Listen," she whispered brokenly, "it's true that when you touch me I go all soft inside. And it's true that's never happened with anyone else. But that's not enough. We believe in different things, vastly different things."

"We're not as different as you might think."

"We're worlds apart, Blake, and you know it. Now will you please take me home to Weatherby House?"

"You're forgetting I live there, too," he said softly.

161

"Not really," she managed, looking at him through tear-blurred eyes. "You belong here. You belong in your modern highrise office building in Sacramento. You aren't living in Weatherby House for the same reasons I am."

"Why am I there?" he asked, crossing the room to stand in front of her. She had the urge to put her arms around his waist and hug herself against him. She had the urge to say nothing mattered but him. But there were principles involved. She knew she was in love with him, but she knew, too, that there were certain things she believed in—deeply—and she couldn't put them aside no matter how much she longed to.

"Since you won't answer, I'll tell you," he said, placing gentle hands on her shoulders. "I moved in to be close to you, to touch you, to get you into my life any way I could. I moved in to make sure you weren't burned out."

She looked up slowly. "I won't be now."

"There's another reason. Sooner or later you're going to have to see that you're in over your head, that you don't have the funds to finish the project, that you never did. When that happens, I want to be there."

Her mouth trembled before she pressed it tightly shut. "Why? So you can bulldoze the place down?"

His eyes flared angrily. "No. So I can pick up the pieces and try to put you back together again."

Her mouth quivered and she gritted her teeth, swallowing. Tears spilled over as she shook her head. "You're wrong," she said.

He sighed heavily, his eyes softening. "Oh, I wish I were. As God is my witness, I wish I were," he said intently. "Carrie, you've been seeing Weatherby House through the eyes of a lonely seven-year-old girl. It's an old rundown Victorian, not some magical fairy palace. And it's definitely not your last bastion."

"You just won't understand," she said sadly.

His hands tightened on her shoulders when she tried to turn away. "I used to look at the place the same way myself when I was a kid, but I grew up. Weatherby House is too far gone. It'll have to come down, Carrie, and I think you're beginning to realize that."

"It doesn't have to come down," she insisted.

Frustration darkened his face. "It's too damned expensive a project to be worth it. There are other places around."

"Not here. Not in Allandale. All this town has is Weatherby House. Once it's gone, that's it. You can't build another like it."

"The first rule of good business is not to let a project become personal, not to confuse feelings with facts."

She shook her head slowly. "Maybe in your business that's true, Blake. Not in mine. In restoration it's very personal. The impossible *can* be done. And yes, it costs money—lots of money—but if that was the only thing that mattered, there wouldn't be a landmark building left in our country. There wouldn't be anything from our past. It'd all be razed. As it is, that's happened too often already."

"Putting that house back together the way it was is

tearing you apart, Carrie. It's too much for you, for anyone."

"Maybe," she admitted. "But I can't let it go. It's part of our past, our lives, part of all of us. We need that. We need the reminders of where we came from, where we've been, to know where we're going. You said it yourself, Blake. You used to look at it the same way I do. Not all of us grow up, Blake. I want Weatherby House to be standing there in full glory a hundred years from now, so some other lonely seven-year-old can stand at the gate and see into the past, can dream a future." She pushed away with determination, swallowing back tears. "I'll wait for you in the car."

Chapter Eleven

When Carla and Blake arrived back at Weatherby House, Mary announced that someone had called Blake from his Sacramento office and wanted him to call back immediately. Blake used her telephone while Carla took the opportunity to escape upstairs to her own work of sifting through the old record files. She could hear the others still hard at work with the power sanders in the kitchen.

Sitting cross-legged on the Belgian rug, she concentrated on reading old letters. The flowery handwriting was difficult to decipher.

Minutes later, the connecting door clicked open, and she glanced up to see Blake standing there, looking down at her. Her heart leaped and she tightened her lips, fighting against her reaction.

"I have to go back to Sacramento for a few days," he told her.

"You don't have to explain anything to me."

His eyes darkened as he came across the room and squatted down, putting a hand along the side of her neck. She knew he could feel the sudden quickening of her pulse as he stroked the base of her throat with his thumb. "When I come back to Allandale, I'm coming here."

She put her hand on his briefly, then let hers drop back to the letters in her lap. "It'd be better for both of us if you didn't."

His fingers tightened, drawing her forward as he lowered his head to kiss her firmly and lingeringly on the mouth. She didn't want to give mixed messages, but after a moment her body seemed to melt toward his, her lips parting as she answered his kiss. He let her go slowly, his eyes glowing. "I'll be back," he said huskily, and gave her chin a light tap with his knuckles before standing. "And I'm going to keep coming back." The door closed quietly behind him.

Carla spent the rest of the day going over letters, papers, and yellowing tax bills. When she came down later, the house was quiet. She found Mary sitting at the dining room table by herself, eating the simple meal she'd prepared.

"Mary, I'm sorry. I got involved in some old files . . ."

But Mary waved a gnarled hand in dismissal. "Never

mind, dear. This is fine and all I want." She was eating warmed-up spaghetti with a cup of tea.

"At least let me fix you a tossed salad," Carla insisted.

"If you're going to have one yourself," Mary agreed.

The kitchen was hazy with sawdust, but a lot of headway had been made in stripping the cabinets. Another day and they'd be done. Carla cleaned a space on the butcher block and set to work tearing crisp lettuce and slicing tomatoes, scallions, celery, and a little red cabbage. She also put on some coffee. When she came back out, Mary was gazing into nothingness, a faint smile on her face.

"You look pleased with yourself," Carla observed.

"Oh, things are working out just fine, I'd say." Mary grinned. There was a mischievous gleam in the old blue eyes, and Carla raised her brows.

"What're you up to, Mary?"

"Sit down and let's have dinner together," she said, waving her hand again.

"Where is everyone?"

"Sam got all spiffied up for an evening in Sacramento. Marv went off someplace in his van, and Michelle took Jacque to the movies." She forked some salad into her mouth and raised her gray brows in pleasure, nodding at Carla.

"Glad you like it." Carla smiled back.

They ate in silence for a moment and then, sipping coffee, Mary watched Carla over the rim of her cup. "You and Blake seem to be getting on like a house afire."

Carla blushed. A quick glance at Mary showed the twinkle in her blue eyes. "Don't you get any ideas, Mary."

The old woman pretended surprise and then chortled. "I shouldn't think I'd have to. Blake seems to have plenty of his own."

"He still feels the same about Weatherby House."

"You'll bring him around, dear. I have full faith in you." She smiled brightly, not the least worried about anything, and Carla suddenly felt depressed. "I've been thinking," Mary went on, studying Carla's pale face. "I should have some people in to appraise my things. I haven't done it in years. There are some valuable objects in the house, you know."

"I do know," Carla said. "It's a good idea. I was going to talk to you about the necessity of packing some of them away until we finish the house."

"We can have them crated and stored in the basement. You're finished down there, aren't you?"

"Yes."

"There's the Benjamin Franklin secretary. I have no idea how much it's worth. Some of his papers are still in it."

"Good lord, you didn't tell me that, Mary," Carla said, appalled. "It should be in a museum."

"It will be. Right here." She sipped more coffee. "I have a few other pieces of equal value, of course. And the carnival glass, Havilland china, and penny glass."

Carla felt faint, thinking of all the treasures that she hadn't even noticed. "But you don't have to worry about all that, Carrie," Mary assured her. "I'll take care of the arrangements. Your job is getting Weatherby House back to the way it was."

The weight of that awesome responsibility worried Carla more than she had let on to the others. Her money was going faster than she'd expected. Marv had found a mill that still manufactured the scalloped shingles, and she had decided to go ahead and order what she needed, rather than burden everyone with the endless jigsawing. The cost would take half the money she had left. Of course the biggest expenses were the basement and the roof. She could pare her other costs, as long as she had her work force. If she ran short, she was sure she could find financing with the project close to completion.

The telephone rang. "I'll get it," she said quickly, dabbing her mouth and dropping the napkin on the table before she headed down the hall to the old wall phone.

It was Roger Deveritch. Carla's regained spirits plummeted at his news.

"I'm not going to make it after all, Carrie. A job came up out of the blue and I can't turn it down. The money's too good, and it'll see me through for a good six months after the job's done. I've got to get back to my art, and this will do it for me."

"That's wonderful, Rog," she said, happy for him but disappointed for herself.

"Look, I'm sorry. I hope you understand."

"You know I do. I was only offering you room and

board. With the economy the way it is, you'd better take real work when you can. Where are you going?"

"Virginia. An old colonial. They're even paying my way back there. It's a private party, apparently. Hey, how's your house coming?"

"We're moving along."

"I'll be back in about four months."

"Well, if you need a project then, give me a call, Rog. I'll still be able to use you."

"Sure thing. Love ya, babe."

Bad news seemed to come in bunches. Three days later Sam received a call and a job offer on a rehab project in Seattle. The money was better than average, and the project sounded as though it would last some time. Carla encouraged him to take it. He was packed and on his way to the Sacramento airport by the following afternoon.

Carla continued working in the upstairs bedroom, which was beginning to come together. The bad plaster had been knocked out, and she'd replaced the decayed braces. After removing the drop cloths, she began work hand-sanding the wood floor. The window hardware was soaking in a chemical solution to remove the many coats of paint. She had removed the window frames themselves and was stripping them, too.

When she was too physically exhausted to do any more work in the kitchen or bedroom, she pored over the old papers from the attic. Sometimes she was up past midnight reading old ledgers and accounts. So far she hadn't located the original plans to the house, which

Mary assured her were in the attic. She did run across several letters from someone named Julia, which referred to some preliminary plans on the addition. She kept these aside, hoping other letters would clarify who Julia was, and what plans she had meant.

Blake returned at the end of the week and things went from bad to worse. Carla didn't even know he had arrived until Michelle came bursting into the upstairs bedroom, eyes bright with excitement.

"I've got an interview on Monday morning with the architectural firm I told you about."

Carla smiled and hugged her. "How? When? That's great news," she said cheerfully, not thinking at that moment of what it would mean to her project.

"Blake arranged it. He knows the big man personally and, after seeing what I've done up here, as well as some plans I had in my portfolio, Blake gave his friend a call, and on his word I've got an interview. I can't believe it! I'm so excited!"

She was hopping around like an older version of her son Jacque. Carla laughed. "I can tell. Settle down, Mickey. Dress conservatively and show off your brains. How can you miss?"

"I'm scared," Michelle admitted, stopping. "What if he thinks my ideas are too . . . well . . . you know."

"He won't. You've got more raw talent than ninety-nine-point-five percent of the architectural majors coming out of the universities. Blake recognized it and he's . . ." She saw a movement from the corner of her eye and turned to see Blake lounging in the doorway, his suit jacket slung over his shoulder. His brows rose faintly, eyes watchful and enigmatic.

"He's what?"

"Fantastic," Michelle cried and hurried over to give him a big hug.

"You've only got the interview, not the job," he said, still looking at Carla. Michelle laughed.

"I know, but at least you got my foot in the door. He'll have a hard time getting it out." She glanced back at Carla, then up at Blake. "I've got to run. Jacque is late, so he's probably gone down to the creek to catch frogs again." She winked at Carla and left.

"It may not work out," Blake said.

Carla turned away, bending down to the floorboard on which she had been working. She took several deep breaths, trying to slow her senses. She hadn't seen Blake for several days, and when he'd appeared in the doorway the force of her feelings had rocked her.

"I interfered," he said bleakly, but without apology. "She may not get the position."

Carla looked up at him. "Did you do it because of me and my work on Weatherby House, or for her?"

His mouth tightened slightly. "A little of both," he admitted.

Carla looked down at the offending floorboard again. She hooked the hammer claw in and yanked. There was a loud shriek of wood and rusty nails as it came free with a jolt. Blake entered the room and stood there waiting. She could feel him watching her, and her depression grew. There was more, and finally she had to sit back slowly on her heels and face it. "Did you have anything to do with Sam leaving?"

"Mary said he went to Seattle," he said quietly, and she knew from his tone that he had been waiting for that question. His answer wasn't as direct as usual. She looked up at him, all the color in her face draining away.

"Did you, Blake?"

He stared at her for a long moment, eyes bleak, mouth flat. "I told him about the project, yes. He said he might write to them about a job. I suppose you could tie the blame for his leaving to me."

Carla's eyes burned, and she lowered her head again, hands clenched in her lap. There was a lump the size of a grapefruit lodged in her chest. She moved along the floor and hooked the hammer claw again. Another board came loose.

"Carrie . . ." He stopped and just the sound of her name spoken in that soft tone made the tears spill out. She kept her face averted. "Go on, say it," he said roughly.

Her shoulders were stiff, and she took a slow, deep breath. She knew what he expected, but he was wrong. So wrong. Michelle and Sam were friends, long-time friends. "Mickey has deserved a chance for over a year," she managed shakily, "and Sam"—she had to stop and swallow hard—"Sam just went through a rough divorce." She shook her head. "What you did will give them a chance to get back on their feet again."

"And you?"

"You knew what it'd do to me," she said quietly and turned to look up at him again. He stood there very pale, hands pushed deep into his pants pockets, his immaculate suit jacket dropped carelessly on a dusty sawhorse. She had the impulse to pick it up and brush it off.

"Do you think that's why I did it?" he asked roughly, eyes glinting.

"You warned me at the beginning that you'd do anything you could to get me out of this project."

His face went white. "If I wanted to cut your work force out from under you, I'd hire Marvin and Mike right now. They're two of the best carpenters I've seen. I could use their skills. They're wasted here."

Her chin came up, eyes sparkling. "Men like Marv and Mike and Sam built this house, Blake. As you say, there aren't many around these days—craftsmen of their caliber, or houses like this one."

"You never give up, do you?"

"Did you think I would? Throw in all the monkey wrenches you can, but I believe in this project. Everything I have is invested in it. Do you think that because a few things go wrong, I'll just throw up my hands and quit? Even if my own beliefs changed, I made a promise to Mary."

Blake frowned. "If it meant ruin to you, she wouldn't hold you to it."

"*I'd* hold myself to it."

"Just like the bearclaws for Marv," he said, smiling

slightly. Carla colored. He looked at her for a long moment, his expression softening.

Her facial muscles jerked with emotion, eyes stinging. He was making a concession for her, and it was one she couldn't accept. "You don't understand yet, Blake," she said in a low, husky voice. "I don't stand in the way of my friends. Good jobs are few and far between. If you have them to offer, hire Marv and Mike."

He looked grim. "How long would it take you to forgive me if I did something like that?" he asked flatly.

"It's business, isn't it? Why worry about it?"

His hands came out of his pockets as his body stiffened in anger. "It's got little to do with business, and you know it!"

She sighed, rubbing trembling fingers on her forehead. "No. You're right." She looked back up. "It has to do with people and their principles."

"And love," he said firmly.

Her heart pounded fast. *Love.* His eyes beckoned her. But it wasn't enough. If she put her beliefs aside for him, she'd come to resent that decision, and him, until it destroyed what trembled so newly between them. In a way, it was blackmail. Give up your project and we can love each other.

"Maybe when Weatherby House is finished and open to the public we can talk about that," she told him slowly, in a wavering voice, as she clung desperately to her inner resolve.

He stared at her. "That's your priority?"

174

Unable to speak, she gave one brief nod. He turned and picked up his coat. She gritted her teeth and clenched her hands tightly to prevent herself from begging him to stay. He glanced back at her once more and then walked out.

Lowering her head, she stared at the old, decayed floorboard. Moving on her knees down along the wall, she worked the claw in again. Blinded by tears, she pulled, and it too came loose with a loud scream.

Chapter Twelve

At dinner that evening it was Carla herself who mentioned the jobs to Marv and Mike. Blake had gone back to Sacramento after seeing her.

"Well, if we're that good, he'll hire us when we're finished with Weatherby House," Marv said between bites of roast beef, mashed potatoes, and steamed vegetables.

"Hey, what're you getting all teary-eyed about, Carrie?" Mike asked.

"You're sure?" she asked them both. "I'm not giving you anything but room and board, and I'm sure Blake would pay well."

"We're comfortable and happy. So what more is there?" Marv responded easily. He nodded to Mike. "Besides, Casanova here has finally found himself a lady. One of the local yokels, no less."

"Shut up," Mike retorted good-humoredly. He

glanced at Carla and shrugged. "What can I say? She's something special."

She grinned broadly. "I never thought I'd see the day, but I'm glad."

"Frankly, I haven't made up my mind yet. I need a little more time."

"What he means is *she* hasn't made up her mind yet," Marv said, pointing his fork at his friend from across the table and laughing.

"Well, while I've got you two here, I'm going to make good use of you," Carla said, her spirits restored.

Marv rolled his eyes. "Meaning what, exactly?"

"We'll start on the roof."

Mike pushed back his empty plate. "May I make a suggestion?"

"Shoot."

"One of the biggest complaints about Weatherby House is the shape the grounds are in. Why not use some of your capital to clean the place up? Get the trees pruned and shaped, till the lawns and put in sod, redo the front fence and gate, plant some flowers."

Marv started to laugh. "Hey, isn't your lady's father in the landscaping business?" The two young men had been friends for a long time and the ribbing was taken in the spirit it was intended. Carla grinned at Mike.

"Now I'm beginning to understand."

"All right, all right, so he's in the business, but the idea is still solid. Those are improvements the town can see happening fast—in a week or two. What we've been doing is inside stuff, resetting the old bones of this ancient skeleton."

It was all too true. Perhaps if the townspeople saw progress being made, they would be less hostile, more willing to listen. Carla looked at Mary, who had been sitting silently throughout the discussion. She had been uncommonly quiet all evening.

"Mary, what do you think?" Carla asked. "What Mike's suggesting would cost a lot of money, money needed for other parts of the project."

Mary looked up and smiled faintly. "I think Mike is right."

Carla frowned slightly. "Are you feeling okay, Mary? You look pale."

"I'm fine, dear, just tired. Those people from the antique guild kept me standing much too long the other day, and then my visit to the attorney depressed me. All that business about last will and testimony makes me feel like I'm getting ready for the grave. And I'm only eighty-four."

Carla looked at Mary's plate and saw she'd eaten very little. "You're sure you're all right?"

"Fine," she said firmly. "Would you help me back to my room? A good nap will do me a world of good."

Carla helped her stand and handed her the cane. She thought she could easily carry Mary herself, the woman was so slight of frame. She looked fragile as a sparrow tonight, as if a small whiff of air would topple her, and Carla felt suddenly alarmed. Then Mary looked up at her, and the old blue eyes burned with a granite will.

She moved slowly along the hallway, and Carla opened her door.

"Come in, dear. I need to speak with you." Carla followed her without question. As Mary settled comfortably on her old recliner, Carla sat facing her on the chair Blake had used that day not long ago. *Blake.*

Mary too was thinking of him, apparently. "Blake won't be back for several weeks," she said bleakly, and Carla thought she knew what was wrong with Mary now.

"I'm sorry, Mary. I hope it's not my fault."

"Partly," she admitted ruefully. "He's in love with you, you know."

Carla blushed and lowered her head.

"He's worried about you, too. He says you're burning yourself out."

"He still wants to buy the property for a new civic center," Carla said firmly.

"He hasn't mentioned that for weeks," Mary replied softly. She leaned far back in her chair, her face showing its age in the lamplight over her head. "He said several things to me before he left. One was that you're continuing with the restoration of Weatherby House because of your promise to me."

Carla stiffened angrily. "That simply isn't true."

"Oh, he said that wasn't all of it. He claims you have some quixotic notion about the house. But he also said you haven't got the funds to finish the project, that you'll use up every cent of your inheritance trying."

"That may be true, but it'll be worth it. When I run

out of my own money, I'll get outside financing."

"Blake thinks that won't be possible."

"Well, that's just one man's opinion," Carla flared.

Mary sighed. "I don't mean to make you angry, dear. It's just that I want to know if I've done you a disservice by saddling you with this old house."

Carla saw the worry in Mary's face, the deepening lines. She stood and came over to her, kneeling down beside the recliner and holding Mary's thin, prominently veined hand. It was dry and very soft.

"Mary, don't lose hope, please. Weatherby House will be beautiful again. It'll be full of life and laughter. People will come from all over to see it and stay here. Please don't lose faith in me."

Mary cupped Carla's cheek with her other hand. "Dear, I'd sooner see Weatherby House bulldozed than have it destroy what I see happening between you and my nephew. You love him, too."

Tears burned in Carla's eyes. "Yes, I love him, but there's more than this house between us, Mary. There's a whole way of thinking about things. It wouldn't work."

Mary sighed, relaxing back. "There should be a way for both sides to win," she said softly.

Carla rose slowly, still concerned. "Can I get you anything?"

Mary opened her eyes. "My knitted lap robe, please."

Carla got the robe and put it over Mary's legs. When she glanced up, Mary's eyes were sparkling mischievously again. "How about a thimble of brandy, too?"

she asked with a wink. Carla laughed softly and brought her that, as well. She leaned down and kissed the withered cheek.

"Don't you worry about anything, Mary. I love you, you know."

"I love you too, dear."

Carla went to the door.

"Carrie?"

Carla glanced back. Mary looked sad, pensive. "Carrie, if you decide to work on the gardens, would you please uncover my goldfish pond? I never mentioned there was one, but it's right there in the front to the right of the cobblestone walkway. I . . . I had to have it covered over a number of years ago."

"After one of your infamous birthday parties." Carla grinned.

Mary's eyes lightened and she chuckled softly. "Yes, well, it was something like your bull and bear-claw incident, but on a much grander scale, I'm afraid. I covered it up to keep the town fathers at bay." She sighed heavily. "I wish I'd told them to go pound sand. There was a fountain in the middle, a pretty maiden pouring water from her pitcher. I used to love to sit on the veranda and look at the pond."

"What happened to the maiden?"

"I had it moved around back into the storage shed, but someone broke in and used a sledge hammer on it."

Carla saw the sheen of tears in Mary's blue eyes. "We'll uncover it for you, Mary. I promise."

Mary smiled up at her. "You know, I wasn't sure you

could do any of what you said when I sold you the house."

"Then why did you do it?"

"A little revenge, I suppose, and I suspected that once my nephew got a look at you, he'd stop spending his life in that Sacramento office of his."

"Mary . . ."

"I believe you can do it," she said firmly. "Against every reasonable argument and in the face of all the opposition, you'll make it, Carrie." Then, before Carla could manage anything past the lump in her throat, Mary grinned and said, "Now would you turn on my television for me, please? It's just about time for that handsome investigator fellow with the mustache. He does my old heart good. Keeps it a-tickin'."

Carla laughed. The telephone rang as she came back out of Mary's room into the hallway. "Weatherby House," she answered with a bright smile.

"So now the house is talking for itself too," came a familiar voice that set Carla's heart racing and her teeth on edge.

"I want to talk to you, Mercer," she snarled.

"Good, because that happens to be why I called."

"Hold on," she snapped and let the receiver drop with a crash against the wall while she made sure Mary's door was closed. Then she took it up again. "Don't you ever again say word one to Mary about my financial situation, do you understand? You worried her half to death with your pessimism and prophecies of doom. So lay off her!"

"I didn't think she listened to me," he said calmly.

"She listened. I've a good mind to pack your gear and drop it off at the Salvation Army."

"It's already gone. I removed all evidence of my habitation this afternoon before leaving."

Despite her anger and against all possible logic, those few words made Carla's heart sink. The silence between them lengthened. She didn't know what to say except "I love you" and "I'm sorry," and she couldn't say either. Not yet. Not now. But the words throbbed inside her nevertheless.

"Was I wrong?" he asked softly.

She squeezed her eyes shut.

"Carrie, I want you in the worst way, and I was beginning to realize that I lacked scruples in how I'd have you. If I thought—"

"You were right," she managed past the growing constriction in her throat. Just the timbre of his voice made her body respond. Thank God he wasn't there where he could touch her, where she could touch him.

"This is one time when I wish you didn't agree with me," he said with a husky laugh. Again the silence grew. Too many words, too many feelings, and all at the wrong time, between the wrong people, she thought miserably.

"Would you still be interested in buying me out?" he asked flatly.

"That depends on how much you asked for it," she said softly. He wanted no connection with her project. He was letting his percentage go, which somehow depressed her deeply. It was a confirmation of his lack of faith in her expertise, in her very beliefs.

"One weekend with me in Sacramento," he told her in a quiet voice that made her heart race and her skin tingle.

"It's too high a price," she murmured huskily, opening her eyes and staring bleakly at the dim walls of the hallway. They badly needed repainting.

"I was afraid you'd see it that way," he said with a sigh. "All right." He named a lower than fair market value price. A bargain.

"You have it," she told him. A quick calculation told Carla she could pay Blake what he asked and still finish the roof, the major inside repairs, and the landscaping. But she wouldn't have enough for the plumbing, rewiring, or cosmetic work. She'd have to seek outside financing to finish Weatherby House after all.

"You're sure you can manage that much?" he asked.

"Were you hoping I couldn't?"

There was a hard silence. "I don't want to be the one to take you under," he said finally, and she could hear the suppressed anger in his tone. "I'll get your papers drawn up." He hung up, and Carla was left clutching the receiver as though it were a lifeline. Her mouth trembled as she replaced it slowly.

Carla called Mike's friend, Ramon Trevino, the following morning and asked him to come by to give an estimate on fixing up the grounds. He arrived an hour later in his neat green truck. He was a heavyset man with the dark good looks of his *Californio* ancestors. Mike had said Ramon could trace his California heritage back five generations to before the Gold Rush, yet some people still thought of him as a Mexican wetback.

He stood with her on the overgrown front lawn, arms akimbo, looking around. "Miss Gelsey, maybe it's unwise business practice to say this, but I've wanted to tackle this place for the last twenty years," he admitted with a faint smile. "I've seen old daguerreotypes of Weatherby House in its heyday. It was really something. All those trees along there were topiaries, and there were flower beds all the way around the house and down the walkways. Over there was a big lily pond with a fountain. There was a maze back behind the house, but that was torn out when the land was sold off and other buildings put up. This place was a landscaper's showcase."

Carla's spirits rose as she listened and watched him. Here was at least one Allandale resident who could envision the house as it was, as it could be once more.

"Can you make it look like that again, Mr. Trevino?"

He glanced down at her. "It'd cost plenty, Miss Gelsey, but I'd give my eyeteeth to try," he admitted with a wink. He named his estimate, which drew a soft whistle from Carla. He shrugged. "Someone else could do it for less by forgetting about the original layout: prune everything back, lay in sod, plant some junipers . . . it'd look all right, but you wouldn't have the same effect."

"No, I wouldn't," she agreed. "Besides someone else

wouldn't have their heart in the work either." She smiled. "I'm looking for people who believe in this project the way I do, who can see what there is here. You've got the contract, Mr. Trevino. If you pare a little off your price, I'll put your sign on the front fence."

"Done." He grinned, eyes gleaming, as he extended his hand and they shook on it. "And the name's Ramon."

Chapter Thirteen

The scaffolding was up and Marv, Mike, and Carla were stripping composition shingles and tar paper from the roof when Blake arrived a week later. She saw his car pull up in front behind Ramon's truck. Two of Ramon's men were feeding cut tree branches into a shredder. The noise was ear-splitting.

When she saw Blake push open the front gate, she worked her way across to the ropes, going down in her unethical manner rather than lowering the scaffolding. She removed her leather work gloves and stuffed them in the back of her dirty coveralls.

Blake's gaze moved over her slowly, raptly, lingering on her hips and breasts before finally coming to rest darkly on her face. "Hello," she said, smiling weakly, wishing she had some control over the rhythm of her heartbeat and breathing.

"Let's talk in the library."

Mary was sitting on the veranda watching everything.

She smiled brightly at her nephew. "Blake, I'm so glad to see you. Will you stay for dinner?"

Blake glanced at Carla.

"You're welcome," she reaffirmed Mary's invitation, and Blake's mouth curved sardonically.

"We'll talk about it," he told his aunt and preceded Carla up the steps. "Business first." He paused long enough to kiss Mary on the cheek.

The library was empty. The old decaying drapes had been taken down and thrown away. The furniture and boxed leather volumes were in storage. The room was filled with light.

"You've been busy since I left," he said quietly.

"We're progressing. There's not much work needed in here. Mainly cosmetics. Repainting, some hand-sanding, decorating." She knew she was chattering, but couldn't help herself. She was so happy to see him, yet so sad as well. She was afraid all her feelings were pouring out of her eyes as the words spilled over.

Blake opened his coat and removed a thick envelope. He tapped it lightly into his open palm before extending it to her. "Here's what you wanted."

She winced inwardly. Her hand shook slightly as she reached out and took it. "Thank you. I'll call the escrow officer and have your money ready."

"Just send your check to my Sacramento office," he told her, hands sliding into his pockets. A muscle worked in his jaw as he continued to look at her with those dark, intent eyes. The impact sent her pulse racing, her stomach muscles tightening.

"Were you at the city council meeting last night?" he asked.

Her eyes widened in dismay. "No, I forgot all about it."

"You should've been there, Carrie. Frank Suraco called me this morning. If you think you've had trouble so far, it's only just beginning."

Her heart pounded in sickening jolts. "So tell me the bad news," she said dryly, pretending not to be overly concerned. But the color was draining from her face.

"They've jumped your taxes to business rates, and they've contacted a high-power attorney to take legal action against you." She closed her eyes. "Carrie, I wasn't at the meeting."

She swallowed hard and opened her eyes again. "Would it have made any difference?" she asked him bleakly.

His face darkened in anger. "Maybe. Then again, maybe not."

His expression made her feel ashamed, yet she knew he agreed with them about her project. It seemed everyone did—everyone who mattered. Even the National Historical Landmark Commission had turned down her application on the grounds that she didn't have enough verification of the house's historic value. She was still going through old letters and records, searching for what she needed.

Everything seemed to be going wrong, even now that the house itself was finally beginning to take shape. Her chest squeezed painfully, and her throat felt dry.

"I'm sorry, Carrie," Blake said softly.

"Not half as sorry as I am," she murmured and then had to swallow again as she looked away from him, embarrassed at how much he was seeing.

He came toward her slowly. When he put his hands on her shoulders, she closed her eyes again.

"I have to go to Denver for a few days," he told her, one hand sliding up along the curve of her neck, lifting the thick braid from her nape. He lowered his head and kissed the soft place where her pulse throbbed, then lightly traced the vein upward with his hot tongue until he reached her earlobe. "When I get back, come to Sacramento for a few days."

She put her hand against his chest and felt the quick beating of his heart. "It wouldn't work . . ."

He moved closer still, and she could feel his hard thighs brushing her softer ones, the warmth of his body drawing her like a magnet. His lips moved to her temple and then trailed down along her jawline. She tipped her head back with a soft indrawn breath.

"Blake, it wouldn't . . ."

He kissed her so softly, so tenderly, that the touch went through her like wildfire. He cupped her face and looked at her. "Come to me for a few days. I've seen what you do, what you want. Come see my side of things, my way. Stay with me."

"I can't. You know I can't," she said tremulously.

"Yes, you can. It's not as though I were asking you to sell your soul."

She shook her head. In a way he was, though obvi-

188

ously that wasn't how he saw it.

"You haven't had a day off since you started," he reasoned huskily, his hands moving down her back to her hips, drawing them against him with a slow, gentle movement that conveyed a pulsating message. "Even the day after you rode Samson." He kissed her again, not allowing her to answer. Then he lifted his head. "You need a few days off. You need to relax. No one works efficiently if they put themselves under too much stress. You need some room to think."

Room to change her mind was what he meant. She clutched the papers. Yet when he kissed her again, her lips parted naturally and her tongue danced with his. She was defenseless against his persuasion. He drew back slowly, eyes black and glowing as he looked down into her face, outlining her cheekbones with his thumbs. "I'll be back by the end of the week. Will you come?"

She closed her eyes and sighed. "Let me think about it, Blake."

He smiled slightly. "I wish you'd give me your promise. At least that way I'd know you'd come—earthquake and national disaster notwithstanding."

She smiled back faintly. "No promises."

His eyes softened, and he smoothed the loose hair back from her temples. "All right, Carrie, but I don't give up any easier than you do." Reluctantly he let her go.

"Will you be staying tonight?"

"I don't think I'd better," he admitted with a slight smile. "All I can think about now is what it's like

189

making love to you, and how much I want to carry you upstairs and lock us in that old bedroom for a day."

She was feeling exactly the same way, and her heightened color and darkening eyes expressed it clearly.

"Thank you for bringing the papers," she told him.

He looked at her, waiting. When she said nothing more, he sighed. "Sure."

He went back outside to the veranda to talk with Mary, and Carla returned to the roof. A few minutes later she heard the roar of his car, saw it pull away from the curb and head down the street. Her throat burned. Turning her head, she saw Marv staring at her with a faint frown. She flashed him a weak smile and then gave her attention back to the shingles.

Carla spent the evening working in an upstairs bedroom. She'd finished the wallpapering and was painting the last bit of molding before moving in some of her own furniture. Near eleven o'clock, she went back across the hall for a few more things before showering. After that, she spent another two hours sitting on her air mattress and sleeping bag going through more papers from the boxes. It was the last pile of boxes, her last hope.

The stack of papers had grown half a foot high when she came across a set of instructions for a prefab house. The date was very faint, but read "March 1851." Frowning, she studied the plans closely. She had read about and seen forms like this before. Prefab houses were nothing new. Many had been done on the East

190

Coast and sent around the Horn by ship during the Gold Rush years. But where had this house been put up? What did it have to do with Weatherby House or its owners?

She kept the form out and put it with the letters mentioning Julia as well as some sketches of Queen Anne additions. Maybe Mary would be able to explain some of these things.

Exhausted, she snuggled down into her sleeping bag and closed her eyes. Everything else put aside, she felt her mind fill with thoughts of Blake. "Come to me in Sacramento," he had said. "Come to me . . ."

She longed to do just that, yet she knew it would only further complicate her life. Being in love with someone didn't necessarily mean that person was right for you. Sometimes being alone was preferable. There was less pain that way.

Coward, her conscience whispered tauntingly. You're just scared to risk yourself again. Blake is no Rob Hanford.

It took Ramon Trevino and his crew a week to cut back the garden. Without the tangled overgrowth, the full impact of Weatherby House's dilapidated exterior was revealed to Main Street Allandale. Carla and Marv sandblasted the wrought-iron fence in front and repainted it glossy black, posting Ramon's business logo and name in clear sight. The hedges down either side of the property line were pruned and shaped to the original topiary design, but it would take some months

191

before they would green up and fill out. All the shrubs and bushes around the base of the house had been cut far back and the gardens turned and fertilized. Planting would come soon.

The smell of overturned earth was heavy as the men began tilling the lawns and getting ready to lay the pipes for a sprinkler system. They found one edge of the covered pond and marked it off.

The shingles arrived by flatbed truck with amazing speed. Payment set Carla back to a dismaying degree, but the roof would be done within a few weeks and then the two biggest, most expensive portions of restoration would have been finished.

Everything seemed to be moving quickly now, including the outpour of her money. What with buying Blake's percentage in the house and the Victorian wood shingles, plus paying for the landscaping, she had scarcely five thousand dollars left. Depressing as she found the idea she would have to seek outside financing to complete the project.

Response from Charles Seder at the local bank and another savings and loan was firm and immediate. *No.* Before packing to leave for Sacramento and more efforts, Carla told Mary about the papers she had found in the attic.

"Well, I'm not sure," Mary said thoughtfully. "I remember once hearing my father say that the house was built in sections, over the years. The last part was done in the twenties by a woman—I think her name was Morgan."

192

Carla's heart tripped in excitement. "*Julia* Morgan?" Julia Morgan had designed and built the famed San Simeon, William Randolph Hearst's seaside castle north of Santa Barbara. Architectural historians had recently discovered other more modest houses built by her as well. One was in Davis, not far from the University of California campus. Her work was revered as original and controversial.

"Yes." Mary nodded. "The name sounds familiar. She stayed here, I believe."

"What part of the house did she build? The solarium?" The design and construction would meet with her known standards, with some minor differences which were probably insisted upon by the owners to conform with the Victorian aspects of Weatherby House.

Mary nodded. "There was a section off the north side as well, but it burned in the forties."

"Oh, Mary!" Carla cried happily. "This may be just what we need. If I have it all worked out correctly, Weatherby House was originally a prefab brought around the Horn in 1851. The core of the house was probably the parlor, dining room, your bedroom, and the library, though those were not their uses at the time. The kitchen could have been a part of the present dining room, where the fireplace and cabinets are now. Then building went on up and around those rooms during the 1880's or 1890's when Victorian designs were all the rage. Later, Julia Morgan came in and finished off the house with the final additions."

"Can you prove all that?" Mary asked hopefully.

"I have the bill of lading for the prefab, letters mentioning a Julia, and I'm still going through the records for more blueprints. If it was Julia Morgan who worked on the house, we may find the plans in her papers at the university. I have a friend who can go through the files and find out but it will take time." She leaned forward and took Mary's hand, smiling brightly at her.

"This may be just what we need to turn everything around. With this additional ammunition, I'll be able to reapply to the commission and get the financial backing I need."

"Not here. Not in Allandale." Mary shook her head, realistic for once.

"Then Sacramento. There are government agencies, banks, savings and loans. I'll talk to them all if necessary."

Mary sighed sadly. "I'm sorry you have to—"

"Don't you dare be sorry, Mary," Carla scolded gently. "Look at how far we've come, and in only six months. Another six or eight and Weatherby House will be ready to open."

"You need more help, more workers, more money . . . more everything."

"We'll do it. Don't lose faith now."

Mary's blue eyes softened with affection as she tenderly patted Carla's hand. "You've worked so hard, dear. So very hard. With everyone against you." She shook her head. "I always thought *I* had a corner on stubbornness and determination."

Carla stood, leaned down, and kissed her. "You take care while I'm gone. No civic disturbances, all right?"

Mary chortled. "All right. If you insist." She held Carla's hand tightly. "You call me as soon as you find a place to stay in Sacramento. I want to know you got there safely."

Chapter Fourteen

After months of work in sawdust, crumbling plaster, and musty rooms, Carla decided to treat herself to a stay in an elegant hotel near Old Town Sacramento. Crossing the street, she walked past the big parking complex and wandered along the boardwalks and through the many shops. She stopped for a yogurt snack and then spent an hour in the Railroad Museum.

During the next week she made the rounds of lending firms, government offices, and banks in a last effort to find financial backing. They all asked the same questions, one of which was why did her own community refuse her loans if the project was so viable. Going over her own financial situation, they found she had gone through a sizable inheritance within less than a year, was in the middle of community and legal disputes, and her only collateral was a half-finished restoration project, power tools, and her old three-quarter-ton pickup truck. With the present market instability, she found that no one was willing to take a risk. Arguing the historic value of the property and her plans to open it as an inn elicited little enthusiasm. Tourist trade was down.

"If you had community support for your project it might be different. Unfortunately, you don't seem to have it," was the common logic.

By Friday she had no choice but to face the inevitable. Donning her jogging suit, she ran until she couldn't anymore. Then she went back to her hotel room and sat, too miserable even to cry. She slept fitfully and the following morning, in a last act of bravado, went to the landscape supply firm and spent eight hundred dollars on a five-foot marble statue of a maiden carrying a water pitcher. It would be delivered Monday to Weatherby House. If all else failed, Mary Weatherby would at least have her fountain and pond.

She was repacking her carry-on bag, putting her toiletries in the bottom zippered compartment, when someone knocked lightly on her door. Thinking it was the maid, she called, "Come in." The knock was repeated and, sighing, she went across the red-brown carpet and opened the door.

Blake stood in the hallway. She gave a small gasp, her eyes widening in surprise.

"I called and Mary said you were here," he told her, his gaze moving assessingly over her face. He frowned. "Are you all right?"

She straightened, her fingers curled tightly around the doorknob, her pulse racing. "I'm fine."

"Mary said you came down to find financing." Before he could ask whether she'd succeeded, she let the doorknob go and turned away.

"Yes, I was just packing to go back," she said quickly, keeping her face averted.

"Carrie . . . ?"

She glanced back and gave a bright smile. "I bought something special for Mary. She . . ." She knew she wasn't going to get the words out and turned her head sharply away, gritting her teeth as tears flooded her eyes against her will. She pressed her lips tightly together and put the last few things into the carry-on bag, zipping it shut.

"Carrie," Blake said again, his voice gentle as he put his hands on her shoulders. She felt his warm mouth against the curve of her neck. "Stay with me for the weekend, and we'll go back to Allandale together and talk to Mary."

He knew she'd failed, and she drew in a shaky, half-sobbing breath. "I still feel the same way about it," she said brokenly, allowing him to pull her back against him, drawing comfort from the way his strong arms closed around her waist and held her securely.

"I know," he said huskily against her hair, resting his chin lightly on her head. "Let's put everything aside for a few days and get down to basics—get down to people and feelings . . . to *us*."

Tears trickled down her pale cheeks, and she found herself wanting nothing more than to do just that. Don't let yourself think about how you've failed, she told herself. Don't think about what you set out to do. Just lose yourself in this wonderful man you love, and enjoy it while it lasts.

Carla leaned back and put her hands over his. She felt their strength, their warmth. "I won't be much company, I'm afraid," she murmured hoarsely. "I'm a sore loser."

"You haven't lost everything, Carrie," he whispered.

She wanted him to kiss her, to make love to her as he had in the upstairs bedroom at Weatherby House, to make her forget everything else. Turning in his arms, she looked up at him, letting him see everything. His breath caught, and his brown eyes darkened until she could see her own reflection staring back at her. Yet when he kissed her, it was with tenderness, not passion. "Are you all packed and ready to leave?" he asked softly, letting her go and picking up her carry-on bag.

She was faintly disappointed he hadn't taken her invitation, yet strangely thankful as well. It showed a sensitivity she hadn't recognized before. She smiled, her eyes moist. "I just have to pay the piper."

Blake drove while Carla stared out the car window in silence. She was too tired to think, too depressed to talk. When he made another turn and slowed, she looked at the elegantly rustic river-house restaurant.

"I'm making an educated guess that you haven't eaten anything since yesterday," he told her, pulling into a small space beside a boat-length maroon Cadillac.

"I'm not hungry," she told him, glancing around.

He turned the ignition off and turned leisurely toward her, sliding his arm along the back of her seat and brushing his fingertips across her shoulder. "Come on, Carrie. Is this the same woman who rode Samson for thirty seconds?" He tugged gently on her long braid.

She looked pointedly around the parking lot filled with expensive cars—half a dozen Mercedes, several Cadillacs, even a silver Pantera! She met his amused glance with a faint raise of her softly arched brows. "I've a feeling you're supposed to be dressed to the nines to go into this place. You look fine in your suit, but I look like someone you just picked up off a freeway on-ramp."

He laughed softly and let his dark gaze travel slowly over her pale yellow-and-green, rolled-sleeved shirt and khaki pants. "You look fine to me. I doubt there's anyone in there who'll object to you once they've had a good look."

She shrugged. If it didn't bother him that she wasn't in a silk dress with alligator shoes and matching handbag, why should she worry? "Okay."

The maitre d' seated them by windows overlooking the river. Just as Carla had thought, everyone was well dressed. There were few women, however, since this appeared to be a lunching place for businessmen. Half of them seemed to be watching her as she crossed the room. Blake said hello to several, stopping briefly to introduce her. When they reached their table, she stared out determinedly at a cargo ship passing by, aware that Blake was watching her. Now that she'd made the decision to stay with him for a few days, she wasn't at all sure it was the best one for her emotional well-being.

You're chickening out, she told herself in self-mockery and turned slightly to meet the full seductive impact of Blake's brown eyes. He smiled.

"Changing your mind already?" he asked, and she found herself not the least surprised that he knew what she was thinking. What had he said about her before? "High-school mentality . . ." Ah, yes, and here she was again, right in character, diving off the high board into deep water when she could barely swim one width of the pool.

She sighed. "No, not really. I've just got the feeling I won't walk away from this weekend emotionally unscathed," she told him, nervously turning her spoon around and around.

His smile softened even as his look became direct and serious. "I'm hoping you won't be able to walk away from this weekend—or me—at all."

Her eyes widened. He reached for her hand, and she quickly retracted it, clasping it with the other on her lap.

"Give me your hand, Carrie," he said, holding out his. "Let's do this right."

"Shhhh . . ."

"Give me your hand or I'll holler what I have to say," he warned, and she saw he meant it. She gave him her hand. He interwove his fingers with hers, staring straight into her eyes. "In case it hasn't occurred to you yet, I love you. I've been in love with you for some time."

Her heart raced. "You've picked an odd place and time to make this kind of declaration, haven't you?" she whispered sharply, glancing around self-consciously.

Blake's eyes lit with amusement. "You know, you didn't blush half this much when I propositioned you," he teased.

The man at the table behind Blake turned slightly to glance back at Carla, and she felt her color heighten even more. She glared at Blake. "Will you keep your voice down!" she hissed, even as her heart and senses reeled.

Blake grinned roguishly. "Maybe I should have started in on you at your hotel when I got the distinct message that you were ready right then to—"

"Shhhhh!"

His thumb stroked hers seductively as his eyes glinted. "We're worth more than another fast tumble. When we make love again, it's going to be someplace special." He raised his brows up and down. "What would you say to the Capitol steps?"

She laughed softly, lowering her head. "I think you've lost your pea-pickin' mind, Mercer."

"Overloaded and burned out in an upstairs bedroom at Weatherby House. What was left dissolved in a hot tub at—"

"Shhhh," she said, squeezing his hand in protest. The man behind Blake seemed to be sprouting ears like a donkey's.

"How about a boat on the Delta?" he asked, brows going up and down again.

She giggled. "Will you please stop it?" She reached across the table with her free hand and planted it firmly over his mouth. "Enough with the ideas, Blake."

His lips parted, and she felt the tip of his tongue trace the lifeline on her palm, his eyes glowing softly as they held hers. He took her hand and kissed her wrist right where she knew he would feel the pounding pulse that gave her away entirely. He smiled, eyes caressing.

Someone cleared his throat and Carla retracted her hand with the speed of a chameleon's tongue picking up a tasty treat. The young, undeniably attractive waiter grinned at Blake and looked solicitously at her.

"Would you like something from the bar?"

"Half a dozen boilermakers." Blake grinned broadly. "She's in need of a little fast courage."

Carla blushed bright red. "No, thank you," she told the waiter firmly and gave Blake a quelling look that should have withered his teasing sense of humor.

"In that case, Danny, we'll make it a magnum of Dom Perignon."

"A magnum!" Carla gasped. "Are you trying to pickle me?"

"All right, a regular bottle should do just fine." Blake smiled, his gaze moving over her in teasing speculation.

"I think I'd better eat something first," Carla muttered, remembering the last time she'd drunk something on an empty stomach.

"Sand dabs are their specialty," Blake said agreeably.

"I'll have lobster," she told him, tenting her fingers beneath her chin and offering him a cloying smile.

"One tail or two, darling?"

"Two." That should set him back about fifty dollars

and maybe shut him up for a few seconds. At least until the waiter left.

"How about oysters for an appetizer? I've heard they're good aphrodisiacs," he commented blandly. The waiter's mouth twitched as Carla's face flamed.

"No oysters, thank you," she retorted.

Blake ordered prime rib with the works. When Danny left, he leaned back comfortably in his chair and surveyed her indignant face. "It's just occurred to me, Carrie, that in spite of my supposedly progressive mind, I'm far more old-fashioned than you are. You have a yearning to return to a romantic, uncomplicated past, yet you'd rather agree to a love affair with me than consider marriage. Would you mind explaining that?" He was smiling as he spoke, but there was an expression in his eyes that told her he really wanted to know.

"You're going too fast," she said shaking her head and hoping he would leave it for now.

He leaned forward again, his voice dropping to a low, intimate whisper. "Not just for you. It hit me like a ton of bricks, as the old saying goes."

She leveled her eyes on him resentfully. "It just wouldn't work."

"Oh, I know that's what you think, but I happen to believe you're as much in love with me as I am with you. Somehow I don't believe you respond to all men who kiss you as though you have rollerskates on your heels."

She blushed angrily and heard choked laughter at the table behind Blake. "It's simple. Blake. We just don't happen to believe in the same things. You believe in tearing things down and building new . . . oh God, Blake, this is all a bad idea," she muttered, eyes suddenly moist. After everything else, this was just about the last straw! "If I'd known you were going to do this . . ." She swallowed hard and stared out the window, trying to regain control of her emotions.

"We could make a good marriage," he told her softly.

"When we're finished here, I want to go back to Sacramento for my truck. I forgot—"

He reached across and turned her face toward him. "You forgot everything the minute you saw me standing in the doorway. Doesn't that tell you something?"

Her eyes filled as she glared at him. "I'm not going to forget everything. I'm not going to forget how and where we met, where you were standing and why!" She brushed his hand away angrily and leaned forward, eyes half-pleading. "Love isn't enough in all cases, and you know it. You've had one bad marriage already. What happens to us a few years down the road when the passion cools and we have to face up to who and what we are, what we believe in?" Her mouth trembled. "You and I are diametrically opposed."

He studied her face for a long moment without saying anything. "You're just plain scared, Carrie."

"Maybe I am," she admitted shakily. It hurt to lose someone. She thought of her mother and father and closed her eyes tightly.

The waiter appeared and prevented her from saying more. The champagne cork popped loudly, and she stared hard at the bubbles in the glass before she picked it up.

Blake held out his glass. "To a lifelong, meaningful relationship."

"And luck in finding her," she said solemnly, touching her glass to his.

"I already have. The problem will be convincing her." His smile was gentle.

Carla didn't think she could eat anything, but the tossed green salad was delicious, and when the succulent lobster tails arrived, she dug in with gusto. She refused anything from the dessert cart.

She felt pleasantly relaxed after a good meal and half a bottle of champagne. Blake had stopped being provocative and was watching her with a faint enigmatic smile.

"Ready to go?" he asked.

"Uh-huh." She smiled. As they were leaving, he put his hand on her waist. When they reached the front lobby, he took her wrist. "Just a minute, honey," he whispered and then approached the maitre d'. They spoke in low voices for a moment and Blake wrote a quick note, tearing it off a pad he carried in his suit pocket and handing it over. Then he took a ten-dollar bill from his clip and handed that across as well. He returned to Carla, and they started for the door.

"Have you got your truck keys handy?" he asked, opening the door for her. Without thinking, she produced them from her shoulder bag. Blake plucked them from her hand and tossed them back to the maitre d', who caught them effortlessly and gave Blake a broad grin.

"What're you doing?" Carla protested as Blake caught her firmly around the waist and ushered her out the door. "Blake, you can't do that! I want my keys back! Now!"

"Shut up, darling."

Carla jerked free and started to march back toward the door into the restaurant. Blake spun her around and pulled her forcefully into his arms, his mouth covering hers in a hard, silencing kiss as she started to tell him just what she thought of his underhanded trick. She struggled angrily, but he only held her closer, grabbing her braid. As his mouth moved over hers, everything inside her came back to life. Gone was the weary exhaustion of the past days, the depression of her failure, the worry about what she was going to do once she returned to Allandale. All she could think of and feel was Blake, his warmth, his strength, his love. She relaxed slowly in his arms, her hands moving around his waist, hugging herself against his hard, wonderful length as her lips parted and she met his growing passion with her own. His kiss gentled, explored, possessed. When he finally lifted his mouth, her head went back, eyes opening slightly. He cupped her face and smiled.

"Just a little something for you to think about while we're driving to my place," he murmured huskily.

"Nicely done," someone said and they turned, confronted by a half-dozen businessmen and two couples waiting to enter the restaurant door she and Blake were blocking. Carla's face burned with embarrassment, while Blake grinned broadly.

"She's going to marry me."

Carla noticed the two women openly admiring Blake while the men were giving her an approving once-over. Blake had a firm hold on her hand as he led her through the parting audience. "I'm beginning to see a definite resemblance between you and Mary," she said through her teeth. "You love shocking people!"

He laughed softly and opened the car door for her. "I know what I want, and I do what I have to to get her."

Carla sat fuming as Blake drove into central Sacramento. He turned into an underground parking lot beneath a highrise apartment building. One look around confirmed his financial status. They went up an elevator to the fifth floor.

When Carla stepped into his apartment, she glanced around in surprise. She wasn't sure what she'd expected, but this certainly wasn't it.

"Did you expect something more ostentatious?" he asked in amusement.

She looked around at the white walls, cream drapes, beige rug and sectional, functional-looking chrome lamps, doe-brown easy chair, and long blondwood coffee table. Even the fireplace was painted white. There wasn't a speck of color in the entire room.

"This is awful." She grimaced.

"That bad, huh?" he asked easily, pushing one hand into a pocket.

"Worse than bad," she confirmed frankly.

"Well, don't make up your mind until you see the other rooms. The bedroom, for example."

"Why do you need a bedroom? Sit in here for a few minutes, and the decor will put you right to sleep."

He laughed softly. "Just take a look around," he said, nodding toward the hallway on the right.

Carla shrugged, then walked across the room and down the hall. She opened the first door on the right. It was an office. There was a drawing board with crumpled papers around it on the floor, a desk piled high, and shelves overloaded with books. Finished mounted sketches were leaning against the wall. She closed the door and looked over her shoulder at him. "Very nice," she said, rolling her eyes before going on to the next.

This room had a bench-press and gravity exercise unit attached to the ceiling. A pair of skis stood in the corner. Tennis and squash rackets were propped against the wall. "Good grief," she muttered, closing that door as well.

"Aren't you going to look at the bathroom?" he asked, opening a door at the end of the hallway for her.

"I'm afraid to," she said under her breath, but did anyway. It was large and glaringly white with tile, more chrome, glass, and mirrors. "At least it's clean."

"And last, the bedroom," Blake said, opening the door on the left of the hall with great ceremony.

"More beige," she said with a soft groan.

"Decorating isn't my forte."

"I'll say. Have you ever heard of color?"

He smiled, eyes glinting. "At least now you can see for yourself how much I need you."

"Oh, no." She shook her head. "You need an efficiency expert for that office of yours, and an interior decorator for the rest of this disaster. You can find both of them in the Yellow Pages."

He laughed softly. "Give me a few minutes and I'll show you what I'm good at."

Carla's face heated as she looked at him with widening eyes. Her heart began to thunder.

Blake grinned altogether too boldly. "Ah. I can see what you're thinking, but that's not what I meant. Why don't you wait in the living room while I change clothes. Then I'll take you out to one of my building sites." His dark eyes took on a roguish sparkle. "Unless you'd rather . . ."

"I'll wait," she said and left.

When he came into the living room, he was wearing faded denims, a workshirt, and tennis shoes. He tossed a sheepskin jacket over the back of the couch. "Why don't you hang your things in the bedroom before we leave?"

"When we get back from the site, I'll be heading home."

He picked up her carry-on bag and walked back down the hall. She followed him. "You're damned high-handed, do you know that?"

He slid the mirrored closet doors open and hung her

bag inside. "I am when I'm dealing with someone who doesn't know what she wants," he agreed.

"I know what I *don't* want. I don't want any part of this!"

"This is incidental. Look me in the eye and tell me you don't want any part of *me,*" he said, walking slowly across the room and stopping right in front of her.

Her breathing became constricted, and her skin felt warm and tingly under his caressing look. She watched his brown eyes darken and glow as they held hers and felt herself go all soft and quivery inside.

"Damn," she whispered.

He put his arm around her shoulders and drew her close as he turned her toward the door. "Something, isn't it? Let's go to my job site before I change my mind."

Chapter Fifteen

The construction site was located fifteen minutes east of the sprawling Sacramento metropolis, a half mile off the freeway, and nestled snugly against the oak-covered hills overlooking the valley. A seven-level skeleton was up and securely surrounded by a high chain-link fence.

Blake unlocked the gate, pushed it open enough for them to enter, then relocked it. A guard emerged from a white trailer, saw Blake, and gave a wave of recognition.

"Everything set?" Blake called.

"Yo!" the man answered.

"Thanks." He raised a friendly hand. Then he turned to Carla with a faint smile. "Up we go, then."

She was looking around with interest. Compared to his home, this construction site was efficiently organized.

"Apartments?"

"Condos," he said, leading her to the lift in the middle of the construction skeleton. He pressed a button, and she could hear the whine of an electrical motor taking them up.

"Four bedrooms, three bathrooms, one with a hot tub, a sunken living room, small kitchen equipped with the most recent paraphernalia, and den. Each unit will have its own private balcony. A recreation complex will be located back there," he said, extending his arm to a leveled section against the hills to the south. "A pool, tennis courts, and clubhouse."

She was more interested in the seven-level structure. "It's similar to your house in Allandale."

He smiled. "That's right. Solar, both passive and active. The concept is to have every possible modern convenience in the way of energy savers and quality safety systems. We've even arranged for a top interior designer to be available to each buyer."

She smiled slightly, eyes teasing. "That's good. Then everything won't be beige or white."

He laughed softly. "Once they sign on the dotted line, they can turn the inside of their home into a bedouin tent if they want."

She had to will herself to look away from him. The

force of his attraction was melting every reasonable thought in her head. She walked across the bare wood-slab floor and looked out. "What an incredible view," she murmured, seeing Sacramento below and beyond. There was a feeling of space, quiet, and isolation, though they were still quite close to the hub of things.

"This one is mine," he said and she felt his strong hands on her hips drawing her back against him as his lips brushed warm against the curve of her neck. She closed her eyes, trembling at the touch.

"How many square feet?" she forced out.

"Twenty-eight hundred."

Her breath drew in as he pulled her shirt free and his hands slid beneath. One moved up, unclasping her bra and then filling with a full breast, the other spread flat over her abdomen.

"Do you like it?"

"Impressive," she whispered and held her breath as his fingertips stroked the hardened peak of her nipple.

"This is where I wanted to make love to you," he told her huskily. "We're standing in the master bedroom."

She put her hands over his, staying the tantalizing caresses. "On a hard floor?"

"Didn't I tell you I was once a Boy Scout?" he whispered, his hands going back to her hips, turning her slightly so she saw a rolled sleeping bag and box on the floor.

"This is a nice setup," she murmured hoarsely, trying to be angry but unable to summon those feelings through the force of others.

"I never leave anything to chance." He released her, and she watched him walk across the floor, lean down, and take up the sleeping bag. He was big, virile, nerve-tinglingly attractive, and it had been a mistake to come here with him because now she didn't want to leave. Why him? Why couldn't she have fallen in love with someone like Marv or Sam, someone with her own values?

The sleeping bag billowed out and then settled in a downy electric-blue cloud. Blake set the mysterious box to one side and looked at her with dark, sensuous eyes. "We'll share a little wine and watch the sunset together."

"And what else?" she asked in a soft yet blunt tone.

"Talk."

She cocked an eyebrow at him.

"Whatever you want," he added softly.

"That's what I'm afraid of," she whispered huskily, frowning. Blake came back, took her hands, and drew her to the sleeping bag. They sat down, facing one another, legs crossed. She laughed softly, nervous.

"Peace-pipe?" she asked.

There was no answering smile. Blake's eyes were serious, intent, watchful. He let go of one of her hands and gently tucked a loose strand of hair behind her ear, then let his fingertips trace her jaw and outline her lips. She closed her eyes with a defeated sigh.

"What're you really afraid of, Carrie?"

"I've told you," she said bleakly, all the laughter gone, looking at him with infinite sadness.

"No, you haven't. Are you afraid to trust me with your love? Do you think someday you might walk in and find me making love to another woman?"

She winced at the staggering memory. "How'd you know about that?"

"Mary."

His hand tightened around hers. "You won't, Carrie. I'm not like that alley cat you were engaged to. I'm a one-woman man, and you're that woman."

"Is that what you told your first wife?" she asked, crying inwardly at her own insensitivity and the need for it.

"It's a fair question," he said slowly. "No, I didn't. In fact, you could say we married for Victorian reasons. We thought we suited each other and then found out we lacked the one all-important ingredient to a good, lasting marriage—love! Luckily, we got out before either of us was lastingly damaged. We're still friends. You can meet her if you want."

"No, thank you," Carla said shakily. The last thing she wanted to do was meet a woman with whom Blake had been intimate. The very thought made her feel faintly nauseous. Jealousy was new to her, and she didn't like it. Her eyes filled as she looked at him. "But here you are about to make another mistake. Love without compatibility."

"Is there anything here that you object to on principle?" he demanded with a jerk of his head. "Nothing was torn down to make way for this project. In fact, in my entire career I've been involved in very little demolition. You can check on that easily enough, if you're willing. Yet you seem determined to believe that's my sole purpose in life, don't you?"

When she didn't answer, he cupped her face, forcing her to look at him. "What I want—what I believe in—is designing energy-efficient, comfortable, safe, lasting buildings that borrow geometric lines from the surrounding environment. I use the best materials, damn the cost. Steel and glass, yes, but also lumber and not the green stuff most contractors are in the habit of using nowadays. Now, how can you say you don't agree with me on the basis of your principles?"

"I can't," she admitted slowly. "But you don't agree with what I do."

"You're wrong," he said gently, thumbs lightly stroking away the tears that trickled down her cheeks. "I admire what you do. I just don't happen to agree with your judgment about Weatherby House."

She closed her eyes. "Well, you're right. I don't have enough money left to finish it."

As he had done before, he took her ankles, straightening her legs, putting them on either side of him, and lifting her so that she fit into his lap. His hands went under her blouse and up over her back as he kissed her neck. "You haven't lost much," he said softly, and she felt his quickened breathing against her sensitized skin. "The land is valuable, and you'll go on to another project."

He still didn't understand, she thought sadly. If only he could see it through her eyes, just once.

"Carrie," he breathed, pressing her closer. "Where are we so different? You want to give people the best of the past and I want to give them the best of the future. We work in the now. See it as all bases covered."

She didn't want to talk. She didn't want to think about anything anymore. That's all she'd been doing: thinking, reasoning, struggling.

"Make love to me," she whispered pleadingly, unbuttoning the front of her blouse and opening it. "Make love to me," she moaned, taking his hands and placing them over her firm breasts.

"God, don't you know it's what I want," he rasped. "But ask more from me, Carrie. Take everything."

She slid her arms around his shoulders, tightened her legs, and rocked against him. He groaned, his hands sliding beneath her, lifting her slightly. His head lowered, and she felt his mouth open over one nipple, circling it with his tongue, then drawing it in to a moist, hot interior as she felt the gentle edge of his teeth. She gasped, back arching, fingers clutching his hair. She felt the blouse being pushed off her shoulders and discarded, along with the loose bra. Then his hands were at the front of her khaki slacks. She unbuttoned his shirt, fingers trembling. His hands slid into the back waistband, stroking the curved, smooth flesh of her hips. Hers moved down, unbuckling his belt, opening his button fly. His breath drew in sharply, and he laughed softly. "What's your hurry?" He pushed her back, rolled her over, and stretched her arms above her head, parting her legs with his as he pressed his hips firmly against hers, letting her feel everything. She looked up at him with passion-drugged eyes, lips parted as her breath came quick and shallow.

"Are you going to take everything?" he demanded.

"No."

"You still just want my body." He smiled slightly and moved provocatively against her, watching her face. Her breath caught.

"Oh, Blake . . ."

"Everything or nothing." He raised up slightly and lowered his head, teasing first one breast and then the other in a gently rhythmic torture.

"No," she groaned, gritting her teeth.

"Yes!" he insisted, and she felt his body trembling. She opened her eyes again and looked up at him, seeing an expression on his face that was her utter undoing.

"Say yes," he repeated raggedly.

"Yes." Her vision swam. "Yes, please."

"About time," he groaned and kissed her. He released her long enough to remove the rest of her clothes and then his.

She propped herself up on her elbows to watch him avidly. "Not only is your apartment pitiful, but you don't know how to fold anything."

He grinned, pressing her back. "I cook a wicked omelet and have been known to wash dishes."

Breath filled her lungs slowly as he entered her, his eyes half-closed. She wanted to slow her response, slow the spiral. "Make it last forever . . ."

Bracing his weight on his elbows, he looked down at

her with glowing, impassioned eyes. "God, I love to watch your face when I love you like this. So beautiful . . . so beautiful . . ."

He brought soft cries from her, and she shook her head, fighting it. "Your security guard is . . ."

"Gone." He gasped. "Scream if you want. I'm the only one who'll hear. Oh, Carrie . . ."

Chapter Sixteen

Carla and Blake drank wine and ate French bread while sitting close together watching the sunset kiss the land in golds and pinks. Blake nuzzled the curve of Carla's neck while inaccurately quoting the *Rubaiyat*. She laughed softly, drawing him down as they made love again, less feverishly this time, prolonging the pleasure, stretching out the time that they were one.

When the night air cooled, they got dressed, rolled up the sleeping bag, took up the box of picnic supplies and went down the lift. Carla dozed as Blake drove back to Sacramento.

Entering his apartment, she felt inexplicably shy. Why did making love somehow seem less intimate than sleeping all night with him, waking up next to him? Blake watched her with a tender smile.

"Are you planning on changing in the bathroom?" he teased gently, and she blushed. He came over and put his arms around her, kissing her lightly. "Go ahead. I'm not laughing."

She took her things from the carry-on bag and went into the master bathroom. She showered quickly and dressed.

When she came out, Blake was standing there in a mid-thigh, dark brown terrycloth bathrobe. "More brown," she groaned and grinned at him.

"What in hell is that?" he asked, looking down her pink, baggy, knee-length T-shirt.

"What I wear to bed," she told him, spreading her arms and pirouetting for him.

He started to laugh. "Where's the satin and lace teddy I was expecting, or the silk nightgown that clings to every curve of your luscious body? Where're the baby-dolls?"

"I like to be warm and comfortable," she retorted. She planted her hands on her hips. "You might as well know now that I sometimes wear socks to bed."

"Argyle?" he managed, still laughing.

"Athletic tube, if you're really interested. Right up to my knees." She looked him over mockingly. "What about you? You're not exactly a page from a men's fashion magazine. That robe looks as though it's seen better days."

"Well, I was going to show some class tonight and wear silk pajamas underneath. Unfortunately, I don't own a pair." His eyes were sparkling, teasing. He started to saunter toward her. "Want to see what I am wearing?"

Her heart fluttered as he stopped right in front of her and slowly untied his robe. Her breath caught as he started to open it, that provocative smile playing havoc with her senses again.

"Boxer shorts?" She laughed when she saw they had small Cupids all over.

"A gift from Aunt Mary," he said dryly.

"Naturally." She laughed and threw her arms around him. "I love you." She kissed him soundly. He held her close for a moment, then stepped back enough to swing her up easily into his arms.

"Let's do this properly, shall we?" He grinned and carried her to the bed.

"You're a stickler for the proprieties, aren't you?" She clung to his shoulders, pretending sudden distress. "Are the sheets clean?"

"Cleaner than the last pair we shared," he said, tossing her into the middle of the bed. He turned off the light and lunged for her, growling suggestively. He pinned her down and kissed her mouth, her eyes, her neck. "At last I've got you just where I want you."

"Lord, haven't you had enough yet?" She giggled. "All I really wanted was a good man who shared my viewpoints, and I end up with an ultramodern glass-and-steel sex maniac!"

He rolled with her until she was on top, her body stretched out on his, and pulled her head down, kissing her again. "Enough?" he said softly. "Never." She could feel just how serious he was.

The telephone rang shrilly, startling them both. Blake hesitated. It rang again.

"Lousy timing," he muttered, and rolled her again so

that now she was beneath him. He stretched out his arm and snapped the light on. The telephone rang again. He caught it.

"Mercer, here."

His body felt wonderfully warm and heavy on hers, and she teasingly stroked his back while caressing his hard calf with her foot. He shifted slightly until she felt evidence of his desire and gave her a hard kiss while shifting the receiver.

Suddenly Blake raised his head sharply, his body going still. Carla looked up at him. His face was pale.

"What did you say?" he said in an odd, constricted voice. He swung himself off her and sat at the edge of the bed, listening intently. "When?" he rasped.

Carla sat up, frightened. She watched him rake a shaky hand through his hair. "No, she's here with me. That's all right. Don't worry. I'll handle it. We'll be there as soon as we can." He hung up and put both hands on the edge of the bed, his knuckles white.

Carla's heart was pounding with sickening thuds. "What is it?"

He turned his head slowly and looked at her, his face ashen, dark eyes filled with tears.

Her throat squeezed tight. "Mary? Is it Mary?"

She saw him swallow. "She apparently had a stroke sometime last night. They found her this morning."

Carla and Blake reached Weatherby House just after two in the morning. Marv, the town doctor, Mike, and his girl were sitting together in the parlor drinking coffee. The girl was pretty, very young, dressed in jeans and a sweater, and clutching Mike's hand tightly as he sat in silence. He looked up at Carla and sighed, unable to say anything.

"We got here as soon as we could. Where is she?" Blake asked in a husky voice, hands deep in the pockets of his sheepskin coat.

Carla felt as though someone were sitting on her chest, keeping her from drawing in a single breath of air. Her eyes burned. Blake had cried before they left the apartment, free-flowing, natural, unembarrassed tears for his aunt. Yet somehow Carla's tears had bottled themselves inside her like a hot, hard lump now congealed in her throat, strangling her.

Just like the day she learned that her father had died in that accident caused by a young drunk driver, and her mother's life was hanging by a thread. Carla gritted her teeth.

"She's in her room," the doctor said quietly, standing. "I didn't think you'd want her body moved until you saw her."

Her body. The words screamed cruelly at Carla. She felt Blake take her hand.

"Thanks," he managed hoarsely. "Carrie?" He looked at her and she saw the question, heard the need, felt what he was saying. She jerked her hand free.

"No," she choked.

He looked at her oddly. Everyone was looking at her. She forced her body straight and looked back. "I'm all right. You go ahead, Blake."

She saw something flicker in his eyes and winced inwardly. He didn't think she really cared. Her icy fingers curled into tight fists as he turned away. Still everyone was staring at her, everyone but Blake, who was walking slowly, painfully down the hall to Mary's room.

Mary! Oh, God, Mary! Mom and Dad and now her, too!

"I'm going outside for some air," Carla said flatly and turned away.

"Miss Gelsey," the doctor said, taking a step toward her.

"Not now!"

She stood on the veranda, gripping the paint-chipped rail until she thought she wouldn't be able to loosen her hands. The stripped garden was filled with eerie shadows. Mary's empty chair was a few feet away from Carla, an open confession magazine still on the seat. The lawn had been partially tilled. One edge of Mary's pond was exposed, but it hadn't been excavated.

Carla let go of the rail and went down the steps. She walked around to the back tool shed and got out the spade. Coming back, she bent to work, flinging shovelload after shovelload of dirt back onto the cobblestone walkway and the newly planted flower bed. Again and again.

"What're you doing?" Blake stood on the steps, staring at her.

"Leave me alone," she said tightly, not stopping, her body shaking with a surge of adrenaline.

He came down the steps and approached. "Stop it, Carrie," he said softly, but she didn't. He stepped forward and reached for her, but she jerked away.

"Don't touch me," she cried out. "Don't talk to me. Just leave me alone." She bit the shovel in again and flung dirt back violently, spreading it across the walkway.

Blake stood watching her, hands deep in his pockets. "I was wrong all the time, wasn't I, Carrie? It wasn't that guy you were trying to get over; it was your parents. That was what made you buy Weatherby House. You told me that yourself. But you didn't say everything, did you?" His tone was so gentle.

She didn't answer as she kept digging.

"Marv just told me you did the same thing when they were killed. You didn't go to the funeral. You sat in the library and studied while they were buried. He said you told him that day that as long as you didn't look at them in the casket, they were still alive. Are they, Carrie?"

Her chest ached. She paused for breath and then pushed the shovel into the earth with her sandaled foot again.

"He said you never let yourself really cry for them. You don't want to cry for Mary either, do you? Why not? Don't you think they all rated it?"

"You don't understand!" she said through gritted teeth, and flung the dirt back. Her eyes felt hot and dry. Her throat was closed, choking her.

"Carrie . . ."

"You leave me alone. Whatever you thought there was . . . I don't want it," she rasped.

"No? You don't want me to touch you, or talk to you, or love you. You want me to leave you alone. All that talk about principles was horse manure. The real reason you didn't want me close was something different. You're afraid some drunk kid might wipe me out on a country road like your parents. Or that I might die of a stroke or heart attack."

"Stop it," she choked.

He caught hold of the shovel and yanked it from her hands, tossing it aside. "That's it, isn't it?" he demanded huskily. He turned her to face him, and her fingers opened and closed. She kept her eyes squeezed shut.

"It hurts too much."

"Life hurts a lot worse without love, Carrie. You don't overcome grief until you face it."

She drew in a ragged breath. "I don't think I can."

"You have to grow up sometime."

Slowly, hesitantly, she raised her tear-filled eyes to his.

Mary's room was softly lit by her reading lamp. Carla closed her eyes tightly as Blake brought her to the side of the bed. She didn't want to open them, but finally she did and looked down at the familiar face of her dear old friend. Mary wore a faint smile. She looked relaxed, slack, hollow-cheeked, but so dear. The covers were drawn up snugly. The lacy edge of her nightgown showed. Her hands were folded on her chest.

Carla put her hand over Mary's. They were so cold, so still. She'd half expected to see Mary's eyelids flutter and open.

"Cry, Carrie," Blake whispered and brushed his lips against her temple. He left her alone. Her throat closed hotly and suddenly the tears came, flooding her eyes and running down her pale cheeks. She knelt by the bed and sobbed. She stayed there for a long time and cried for more than Mary Weatherby. She cried for her mother and father. They *were* gone. Ignoring the fact didn't change it. Yet they weren't dead to her. They never would be. Neither would Mary.

When she came out, Blake and the doctor were standing at the front door talking to an ambulance driver. Blake turned and saw her. He pulled her close, stroking her hair. "A warm shower, a glass of brandy, then bed," he whispered. "Come on, honey." He looked so drawn and pale, but still he had a smile for her.

They went up the stairs to the top floor. He started to open the small bedroom, but she shook her head. "I've moved back into the other one."

"You can't stay in there."

"It's done." She opened the door, went in, and across to her antique Victorian dresser which she'd taken out of storage and had shipped. "I'll be back in a few minutes," she murmured huskily.

When she came back in her cotton pajamas and long terry-cloth robe, she found Blake standing in the middle of the room, hands on his hips. He was turning around slowly, studying the replastered and cream-painted ceiling with the painstakingly re-created decorative molding of flowers and leaves, the refinished wood trim, the restored walls papered now with a soft Victorian rose print, the hand-sanded varithaned floor partially covered by an antique flower-pattern rug. His pensive gaze traveled on to the stained-glass windows, down to the other clear windows lightly covered with Nottingham lace and satin pull-back drapes with golden rope tassels.

He looked at the queen-sized bed with its hand-crocheted lace canopy and the worn but still charming wedding quilt Carla had bought at a garage sale for twenty-five dollars from an old woman who'd seen how much she admired it. He went on to look at the commode, the cut-glass lamp with brace stand, the porcelain pitcher and bowl, the highboy, the dresser with its three-way beveled mirrors. Everything fit perfectly into the room that still smelled faintly of new though seasoned redwood, plaster-of-paris, paint, and varnish.

He turned slowly and looked at her. "I didn't think you could do it," he murmured. "I was wrong."

"No," she admitted softly, "it's only one room."

"It was the worst in the house." He looked around again and sighed, a faint smile touching his firm mouth. "It's new, like it was just built yesterday, but I feel as though I've just stepped back in time a hundred years."

Her eyes filled again. She'd thought she was all done

with crying. "That's the way you're supposed to feel. It's what restoration is all about—giving you a sense of the past, a chance to touch it again." She looked around as well. "I can't prove it, but I believe the core of Weatherby House came around the Horn as one of the first prefabs during the Gold Rush. Later the other rooms and third floor were added, as well as the gabled roof and turrets. Mary . . ." Her voice softened sadly. "Mary remembered a woman named Julia Morgan working on a solarium in the twenties, and a north addition—but it burned down later."

"All of which would make Weatherby House of historic interest, a landmark."

"But as I said, I can't prove it. The letters and records are too sketchy." She sighed. "Mary's gone. I'm out of money. Allandale has filed legal action and . . ." She shook her head and spread her hands helplessly, eyes wetting. "One more day and at least Mary would've seen her fountain back," she managed in a watery, choked whisper.

Blake looked at her tenderly and then gazed around at the restored room in all its Victorian glory. "All right, we'll finish the house. Consider it my wedding gift."

Carla's heart seemed to stop beating. She stared at him. "You mean it?"

"I never say anything I don't mean," he told her, and walked across the room slowly until he was right in front of her. He put his hands on her shoulders and looked down at her seriously. "I said I love you. I said I want you. I said I need you. I meant every word."

Her eyes softened and glowed. She smiled. "You said Weatherby House was a lost cause. You were absolutely right about the cost. Do you know what you're getting yourself into?"

"I love a woman who can admit it when she's wrong. But you were right when you said it could be done, and that it'd be worth it."

"Isn't it wonderful when both of us can be so right?" She hugged herself against him and thought of Mary. "Oh, Blake, I love you so much," she murmured huskily and heard his heart quicken, felt his arms warm and strong around her.

Chapter Seventeen

Carla selected an apricot polished-linen business suit and a creamy silk blouse set off with classic wheat pumps for her appearance before the city council. She wore her waist-length hair in a neat chignon rather than its usual long braid. A quick last glance in the full-length Victorian mirror confirmed that she looked every inch the successful businesswoman. She smiled faintly, hoping the image might do some good.

Blake had tried to argue her out of addressing the meeting. "The town's animosity is still running high against you," he said, but she had insisted he stay out of it. With Mary's death, the council had decided to go ahead with its legal action and, rather than wait for the attorney to come knocking at her door with papers,

Carla had decided to face them head-on one last time.

When she opened the door to the meeting room at City Hall, Mayor Suraco looked dismayed. He glanced down the table at Cynthia Seder, who had a smug smile on her pinched face. Next to Mrs. Seder sat a gray-haired, distinguished-looking man with a black leather briefcase lying on the table in front of him. Undoubtedly the attorney, Carla thought, glancing toward the end of the table where Blake was sitting, watching her grimly. He raised his brows faintly in question, and she shook her head once.

People had turned in their chairs to look at her and then turned away, whispering among themselves. Sitting in one of the front rows, Carla recognized her old buddies from Bronco Sam's—Frank, Terry, Floyd, and Jack. Frank raised his hand to her, and she was grateful, even while knowing they all hoped she'd be closed down so the civic center project could begin.

Drawing in a deep, calming breath, Carla walked to the front and took a seat. She felt all eyes on her, heard the hostile murmurs, and saw Suraco's nervous jumpiness. Poor man, he probably thought they were going to lynch her, she thought with wry amusement.

The meeting began and progressed swiftly. Everyone was there to witness the end of an era. When the subject of Weatherby House was opened, Carla stood up. "I'd like permission from the Chair to address the meeting," she said quietly. Suraco's face reddened as he glanced down the table at Blake, Cynthia Seder, and the blank-faced attorney, who had unsnapped the lock on his briefcase but hadn't yet opened it. Suraco looked back at Blake and a silent message was passed.

"Go ahead, Miss Gelsey," Suraco said, sitting down slowly.

"Hey, wait a minute," someone cried out from the audience. "She turned this place into bedlam last time."

"Yeah! Let's get on with it! Close her down and—"

Suraco pounded the gavel, perspiration beading on his forehead. Blake stood. Carla could tell by the set of his broad shoulders and the dark glint in his eyes that he was well on his way to a show of temper. If he said anything, the meeting would turn into a riot. Someone would surely bring up the fact that he had stayed several nights at Weatherby House, had even moved in for a while, and that his championing of her was less than impersonal. He looked at her and she gave him a pleading look for silence.

The people in the room had quieted, interested in what Blake might say. Some of them were twittering like magpies. Carla kept her head high and didn't sit down. Rather, she plunged in while she had the chance.

"Several months ago I spoke to this assembly in a tactless, irresponsible manner and I'd like to apologize for that. There were many things of which I wasn't aware at the time, many difficulties facing Allandale— the unemployment problem, the loss of several large business concerns, and the slow downward spiral of population. Those are facts of which I should have apprised myself before presenting my own proposal."

"I'll say!" someone shouted from the back. "Just

231

close down and get lost! You and those other hippies!"

Terry shot to his feet. "Shut up back there! The four of us up here are out of jobs because of Miss Gelsey, but we're listening. The rest of you sure as hell can, too!" He looked embarrassed after his outburst and sat down, red-faced. Carla smiled at him. Suraco had his hand over his eyes, as though he were fighting a tension headache. Blake's lips were white, and a muscle worked in his jaw.

"You have the law on your side," Carla went on and looked briefly at the placid-faced attorney waiting his turn. She faced the assembly of townspeople glaring at her. "You can close me down. Your tax increases, and various other pressures you've already brought to bear, might eventually do that anyway. But I'm here to ask you not to." She went on to briefly outline the historical information she'd found on the house.

"The other problems still exist and, as Mr. Mercer told me, people are more important than old houses. You need a civic center. You need jobs. You need a library. You also need to hold on to your history. With a little juggling, I think we can do all of those things.

"A half-mile outside town on the hills southeast of the country club, there's a section of land that's been for sale almost five years now. It would be a perfect site for your civic center. If you tore down Weatherby House and this old City Hall, you'd still need more space for parking, either under the building or taking up the side streets. By putting the building outside of town, you would have plenty of space around it for parking as well as for spotlighting Mr. Mercer's architecture—like Frank Lloyd Wright's Marin County Civic Center, anyone passing on the freeway would see it.

"This City Hall could be restored and converted into a library and Gold Rush museum." There was a low rumble of surprise at that suggestion. "As for Weatherby House, I want to open it to the public immediately. I made a mistake taking on this project as *mine*. Weatherby House belongs to all of us. It's part of our town's heritage. I should've made you feel part of what we're doing there, instead of alienating you at the beginning. I want to rectify that, if you'll allow me to. If anyone here tonight is interested in a walk-through to see what's been done, how far we've come in just six months, you're welcome, anytime. Right after this meeting, if you'd like. I am not, contrary to public opinion"—she smiled—"running a hippie commune on Main Street." There was mild nervous laughter.

"I've recently been promised additional funding to complete the restoration of the house." She looked at her four drinking buddies. "If you four gentlemen would like jobs, and you have no objection to working for a woman, you have them, effective this evening. Union wages." She winked. Frank laughed.

There was more talk among the assembly, less hostile now, more interested. She took a last deep breath. "All I'm asking is that you delay your decision on this matter for another week, that you walk through Weatherby House. People will come to see it, to stay there. They'll come to see your Gold Rush museum. They'll drive by and see your civic center, an indication of a growing town. They'll eat at your restaurants, buy at your stores. It's possible to have the best of two worlds. There's only one Weatherby House and it's here, in your town. Please don't tear it down." Her voice broke at the last and she sat down quickly.

Amazingly enough, it was Cynthia Seder herself who moved the meeting be adjourned to Weatherby House.

Carla had earlier proceeded on high hopes and had had Ramon Trevino string the grounds with lanterns and put a pair of spotlights on the house itself. Mary's fountain had been uncrated and set in place, though the pond was only partially excavated, reminding some of the old-timers of Mary's indiscretion many years earlier. Carla quickly divided the assembly into three parties. Marv and Mike, dressed in sports jackets, slacks, and ties, took their two and she took the last. They had organized it so that each tour would end in the upstairs bedroom.

By midnight, everyone had been through the house, seen the work in progress, and been refreshed with cold drinks and hastily assembled hors d'oeuvres. Now they were on their way home, hopefully with softened hearts.

Cynthia Seder was one of the last to leave. "You know, I'm almost embarrassed to admit it, considering my position in the matter, but I was always intrigued by this house. I always wanted to see the inside. Nosy, I guess." She smiled and touched Carla's arm. "You have my vote."

The attorney gave her a wry though admiring smile. "Very neatly done, Miss Gelsey. I think you've done me out of my case."

"I hope you're right," she admitted frankly.

He laughed easily, took a business card out of his pocket, and handed it to her. "When you're ready to open for business, give me a call. I'd like to bring my wife up here for a weekend."

As the gate closed on the last guest, Blake put his arms around Carla's waist, drawing her back against him. Ramon shut off the lanterns and spotlights, casting the grounds into shadowed darkness. She could hear Marvin's stereo go on as he and Mike and Mike's girl began celebrating.

Blake kissed the curve of Carla's neck as she relaxed against him. She sighed.

"Come home with me," he whispered huskily.

She smiled. "Just let me get my nightshirt."

"You don't need it."

They drove to his house at the country club. It was warm, but he started a fire anyway. "Atmosphere." He grinned, pouring out two glasses of wine and then sitting down next to her. His suit jacket, vest, and tie were discarded and the top buttons of his shirt were opened. Carla's jacket was off and her pumps on the floor.

"You had a few extra things left up your sleeve, didn't you? Frank Lloyd Wright, indeed," he growled, his eyes belying his tone. "Don't get any wild ideas about me helping you fund restoration on that dilapidated City Hall."

She smiled over the rim of her wineglass. "Ah, Mr. Mercer, and I thought I'd brought an end to your search-and-destroy missions."

"In one case, yes. Hmmm, but under certain conditions . . ." he said, putting his glass aside and moving closer to her. "I have a few surprises left for you, too, Miss Gelsey," he said with a roguish grin.

She, too, set her glass aside and snuggled close, putting her arms up around his neck. She raised her brows. "Have at it!"

He laughed softly and pulled the pins from her hair, letting it fall down her back. He began to unbutton her silk blouse. She smiled, tracing his ears with a teasing finger.

"It seems Aunt Mary wanted everything neatly tied up," Blake told her huskily, laying Carla's blouse open and running his index finger lightly along the lacy edge of her slip. "Her attorney took me aside this evening while you were giving your grand tour. We're both to be at his office tomorrow morning, nine sharp, for the reading of Mary's will."

"Both?" she repeated, finding it hard to concentrate as he took off her blouse and lowered the satin straps of her slip.

"I managed to get some information out of him," he went on. "Mary changed her will a few weeks ago, making you her major beneficiary."

Carla drew back. "Oh, Blake, I didn't—"

"Shhhh," he said, putting a finger to her lips and smiling at her. "She wanted you to finish the house and she made provisions to see you'd have the money you needed."

"But you . . ." she managed huskily, searching his face carefully, afraid she'd see resentment there.

"I have all I need, and she knew that. It was a bone of contention between us, in fact. I didn't want the house, and what would I have done with all that bric-a-brac?"

"You call Havilland china, penny glass, and Wedgwood *bric-a-brac?*" she teased softly.

He brushed her hair from her temples tenderly. "The point was to see you got your dream, Carrie. It's what I want, too."

"Everything will be the way it was at Weatherby House," she said, her eyes filling.

"I think she knew that." He kissed her softly, parting her lips with his tongue. After a long moment, he raised his head, his breathing heightened. "Now, do you want to make love in here on the rug in front of the fireplace or shall I carry you down the hall to my bedroom?"

Her body warm and quivery, Carla stood up slowly and took off her remaining clothes as he watched with darkening eyes. "Right here," she whispered, sitting down and patting the rug. She watched as he undressed as well. He dropped down beside her, his hand making a sweeping caress from her thigh up over her hip, from her waist to her breast. "Right now," she sighed, closing her eyes slowly and drawing him closer.

"Something else," he murmured as his body covered hers, and she opened herself to him.

"What?" she moaned softly. He ran his tongue along

her collarbone, making her flesh shiver and her nipples tighten into hard buds. She moved her hips in a slow circle and heard him catch his breath. He leaned more of his weight against her to stop the arousing movement for a moment longer.

"Mary left us a letter," he said and smiled wryly down at her.

She smiled slightly. "And you want me to read it right now?"

"Not necessary," he said huskily, moving very slowly, teasing her. "It was short . . . concise . . . to the point."

"Well, don't stop now," she managed shakily.

"She said"—he paused to draw in a breath—" 'If the two of you stubborn fools don't get married, I swear I'll come back and haunt you both.' "

Tears came. Carla laughed softly. "Well, Mary Weatherby always did get her way, didn't she?"

Center Point Publishing
600 Brooks Road • PO Box 1
Thorndike ME 04986-0001 USA

(207) 568-3717

US & Canada:
1 800 929-9108